AMERICAN LAW ENFORCEMENT
VS.
THE RUSSIAN MOB

THE DRUG WAR; GOING AFTER THE BIG BOYS!

LEONARD C. LEE, SR.

authorHOUSE®

AuthorHouse™
1663 Liberty Drive
Bloomington, IN 47403
www.authorhouse.com
Phone: 1 (800) 839-8640

Published by AuthorHouse 02/14/2019

ISBN: 978-1-7283-0064-1 (sc)
ISBN: 978-1-7283-0062-7 (hc)
ISBN: 978-1-7283-0063-4 (e)

Library of Congress Control Number: 2019901853

Private investigator J. W. Walters answered his ringing phone. "Hello. J. W. Walters speaking."

"Mr. Walters, this is Detective Susan Littleton, Robbery Division. I'm calling you regarding the ten thousand-dollar payment that you received from the late Deacon Fred Smith. The police department expected you to follow up with us by turning in that money since we informed you that it was stolen."

Walters, nervous, was not exactly sure how to respond. "I've been somewhat busy lately, and it slipped my mind. But if I remember correctly, I thought you actually said that you were not sure the money was stolen."

Detective Littleton didn't want to hear any excuses. "You still haven't explained to me when you plan to arrive at my office with that money."

"Detective, I was paid this money for services rendered, and I think it's unfair for you to request money from me not knowing if it's actually stolen money. But if you insist—and because I've always cooperated with law enforcement and considering I've always had a good relationship with you guys—I'll bring it in tomorrow."

"Tomorrow is not good enough, Mr. Walters, because you're already overdue. You need to turn that money in to me today." The detective hung up the phone.

An hour later, J. W. Walters arrived at Detective Littleton's office and submitted $10,000 cash. "When can I expect to get my money back?"

"If the money is stolen, you're not going to get it back." As he was about to leave, she asked him to have a seat. "Are you aware of what a class E felony is?"

"No, not exactly."

"It's a crime that carries, at a minimum, a sentence of four years in prison. So when you knowingly or unknowingly accepted that stolen money, you aided in covering up the theft. You could also lose your investigator's license."

The thought of losing his license frightened Walters, so he thought he would try to defend his actions. "The guy didn't tell me the money was stolen."

The detective did not appreciate his response. "With all the news on TV and in the newspapers in this city about the deacon stealing from his own church, you had to know he paid you with stolen money. Plus, you previously said to me and Detective Virgil Phillips that people don't routinely come to your office with ten thousand dollars cash. You do remember saying that to us, don't you?"

"Yes, I do. But I'm telling you, Detective Littleton, if I'd known the money were stolen, there's no way I would have accepted it. I've run a legitimate business in this city for years, and I don't have a criminal record. It's important to me to keep my business clean."

Detective Littleton had heard that line before and let this perp know it. "We just had a lawyer who'd practiced law in this town for forty years commit two murders, so don't tell me how long you ran a clean business. I'm going to talk to the assistant district attorney about this, and how she wants to proceed is completely out of my hands."

J. W. Walters got up from his seat and headed out the door. Detective Littleton went directly to the office of Assistant District Attorney Maria Sanchez to discuss Walters's situation.

When she arrived, ADA Sanchez was reviewing documents from one of her cases. "Come in, Detective Littleton. What can I do for you today?"

"There's a private investigator by the name of J. W. Walters. He was hired by a man that we just put in prison for theft and murder, Deacon Fred Smith. He paid Walters ten thousand dollars cash for his services. The problem is that there's a good chance Deacon paid him with stolen money. Walters claims that his client didn't inform him that it was stolen money."

ADA Sanchez quickly replied, "So a man walks into his office and gives him ten thousand dollars cash at a time when there's an ongoing high-profile trial with theft as a key issue. Does he think we're sleepwalking? If Walters had done his due diligence on that money and properly reported it to our office, maybe District Attorney Barbara Davis, Fred Smith, and Dick Overton would still be alive. I want him arrested immediately."

"I will do it."

Meanwhile, J. W. Walters had returned to his office and was sitting at his desk when his phone rang.

"J. W., this is Pete Johnson, and I expected to hear from you before today. Where's my money?"

At the sound of Pete Johnson's voice, Walters got very nervous and began to sweat. "I just delivered ten thousand dollars to the police because some guy hired me with stolen money."

"But J. W., what about the money you owe me?"

"Pete, you know I've always paid you every dime I've ever owed you, and you'll get this money too."

"If I don't get that money this week, the man I work for won't be as nice as the police."

"There's no need to make threats, Pete." Walters was intimidated but didn't like being pressured.

Upset, Pete Johnson warned, "Oh yeah. When you don't pay me on time, that damn money comes out of my pocket. And since you're late, you bring me fifteen thousand."

Angrily, Walters replied, "I just told you that the police took all the money I had to pay you. And I don't need all this stress from you. As soon as the police give me my money back, I'll bring it straight to you."

Suddenly Pete Johnson exploded in anger. "Oh yeah? I'll show you stress. I'm on the way to your office, and you better be there when I get there!" He slammed the phone down, rushed to his car, and headed to Walters's office.

One of J. W. Walters's best-kept secrets was his love for heroin, and that was how he came in contact with Pete Johnson. Johnson, an under-the-radar guy in the local opiate trade, always wore a Colt .45 in a shoulder holster concealed under his jacket. And he was very dangerous. Walters planned to pay Pete Johnson by overcharging Deacon Fred Smith for his services, but the detectives spoiled his plan when his name came up during their investigation. And now they had confiscated the money, and he couldn't pay Johnson, who was on his way to get satisfaction.

Walters had prepared for Johnson's arrival. He had no plans of giving him money. And high on heroin, he was in no mood to be pushed around.

At about six forty-five Wednesday night, Johnson arrived. Walters owned two handguns and a shotgun; the shotgun lay concealed across his lap as he sat in a chair behind his desk.

Johnson walked into the office and sat in a guest chair in front of Walters's desk. "I'm here for my money."

"Pete, I told you the police took all of my money, and I'm trying to stay out of jail. So I don't need you coming over here acting like Al Capone."

Johnson jumped to his feet. "You son of a bitch, you owe me money!" Johnson suddenly reached for the .45 and took it out of his holster.

But before he could aim and shoot, Walters raised the shotgun, pointed it at Johnson, and pulled the trigger. *Boom!* The blast was so powerful that it knocked Pete back. He fell over the chair to the floor, dead.

Then J. W. called the police. "My name is J. W. Walters, and someone just tried to rob me at my office. I shot and killed him. My office is located at 317 West 56th Street."

Police dispatch immediately sent out a call. "J. W. Walters has reported an attempted robbery and a defensive shooting at his office, located at 317 West 56th Street. All cars in that vicinity proceed to that location."

When officers arrived, Walters was standing on the sidewalk outside his office. After checking Walters's identification, the officers began to secure the crime scene. It wasn't long before the detectives arrived. Homicide Detective Michael Corns and Detective Littleton, who happened to be at the station when the dispatcher made the announcement, were there to work the scene. A representative from the coroner's office and several other officers arrived on the scene.

Detective Littleton read Walters his rights. "J. W. Walters, you have the right to remain silent. Anything you say will be used against you in a court of law. You have the right to an attorney. If you cannot afford one, an attorney will be assigned to you. Do you understand the rights that I have just read to you?"

"Sure, I understand what you read, but why are you arresting me? I told you the guy was trying to rob me."

"I'm not arresting you for the shooting. I'm arresting you for theft by receiving."

Two officers put Walters in a police car and took him to jail.

Jail might be the safest place for him considering the person he'd just killed and his involvement in the local crime organization. In this city with a population of nearly 750,000, the opiate business was on the rise, a lot of money was being made, and the number of crimes was increasing. The local law enforcement professionals were about to face their greatest crime-fighting challenge.

The following morning, Detective Michael Corns informed his lead, Detective Virgil Phillips, of the fatal shooting of Pete Johnson by J. W. Walters. Phillips also received a call from Detective Littleton.

"Last night, ADA Maria Sanchez ordered the arrest of J. W. Walters for receiving stolen money from Deacon Fred Smith. My team is also securing a warrant for Walters's home and office. We're also getting his phone records. I'm sure you've been informed of the shooting that occurred at his office last night."

"Yes, Detective Corns informed me about the killing. What do we know about the victim, Pete Johnson?"

"We don't have anything on Pete Johnson yet, but I got the impression Walters wants to talk about something. Prior to the shooting, he seemed a little unsettled. Also he used a shotgun to kill Johnson. So if you're being robbed, how do you have time to pull a shotgun out of your closet? Pete Johnson had a .45 and didn't get off a shot."

"You think Walters was waiting on this guy?"

"As soon as we get those phone records, we'll be able to answer those questions. I was thinking you and I could tag-team Walters and see what we can get."

"I'm in."

Detective Littleton made a call and had J. W. Walters moved from his cell to interrogation room one, and she and Detective Phillips proceeded to that location.

Detective Littleton opened the discussion. "Mr. Walters, our records show that you've never served time."

"That's true. I have an honest business. I always have, and I always will."

"But now you're looking at four years in prison."

Walters thought he was a victim. "This is my first offense, and even if I am guilty—and I'm not saying I am—why should I have to do the full four years for my first offense? Why?"

Detectives Littleton and Phillips were surprised to see the nervousness and obvious body language of Walters.

"Detective Littleton, can I have a word with you?"

They stepped out of the room as Detective Phillips continued, "Did you notice his temperament and body language?"

"Yes, I did. This man's a junkie."

"Do you think that shooting last night was drug related?" Detective Phillips asked.

"Something is going on. Here's a man with no criminal record accepting what he had to know is stolen money, risking his business and his freedom. And then he kills a guy with a shotgun and claims that the guy was trying to rob him."

Detective Phillips made a recommendation. "Let's hold off on further questions until we get the phone records and confirm whether he knew the guy he killed."

"Yeah, I agree." Detective Littleton then instructed the two officers waiting in the corridor to take Walters back to his cell.

Detective Phillips thought this had become a homicide and drug case. "We need to get narcotics involved, and maybe they'll have something on Pete Johnson."

Detective Littleton agreed. Detective Phillips called Detective Bobby Mitchell, head of Narcotics division.

"This is Detective Virgil Phillips and Robbery Division Chief, Susan Littleton, is also here. We've got a couple of cases going, and there's some indication that drugs may become a factor in our investigations. We'd like to meet with you to see if you're familiar with the men we're looking at."

That got Detective Mitchell's attention. "Sure, come on down."

Detective Phillips and Littleton headed to Detective Mitchell's office.

After arriving, Detective Littleton opened the discussion. "We've arrested J. W. Walters on a class E felony. He's a private investigator who received ten thousand dollars of stolen cash as a payment for his service. We've got him on that, but last night in his office at approximately seven o'clock, he killed a man by the name of Pete Johnson with a shotgun and claimed Johnson was attempting to rob him. Detective Phillips and I had a meeting with Walters today and noticed he appears to be in need of a drug fix. That's when we decided to end that meeting, get his phone records, and try to establish prior contact with the man he killed."

Detective Mitchell was very interested in the drug connection. "We've got an opiate explosion in our city, and we're working a number of suspects. That name Pete Johnson sounds familiar. Let me check a file." He got up from his desk and stepped to his file cabinet. "No, I got a Pete Williams, but not a Pete Johnson. I'm documenting Johnson and Walters. I'll have my team double-check our database, and if we get anything in the future, I'll call you."

Detective Phillips reasserted future cooperation. "Ok, Bobby, we wanted to fill you in, and if we turn up anything on drugs, we'll let you know."

Detectives Phillips and Littleton went back to their offices. Detective Littleton got a call from a robbery team member, Betty Baker, who had been leading the search of J. W. Walters's home and office.

"This is Detective Baker. We didn't find anything at J. W. Walter's home, but we did find a small quantity of drugs at his office, which we've confirmed to be heroin."

Detective Susan Littleton wanted more information. "How did you confirm that it is heroin?"

"We contacted one of our narcotic experts, Dorothy Butler, and she conducted a field test. She provided a hard copy report of the test results."

Detective Littleton was pleased with the news. "Great! Please email me a copy of that report as soon as possible, and make sure that you protect that evidence per our standard operating procedure. Thank you."

Detective Littleton ended the call and immediately called Detective Phillips. "This is Littleton, and we've found heroin in J. W. Walters's office."

Detective Phillips was pleased but not surprised. "Drugs at a crime scene. Just like we suspected. This guy is an addict. And I strongly believe those phone records are going to confirm that he and Pete Johnson have a history."

The detectives saw their case coming together.

"Phillips, we should have something on those phone records tomorrow. And the next time we talk to Mr. Walters, we'll be able to have a very thorough discussion."

"Also based on the reports I'm getting from my team, the crime scene resembles a shootout more so than a robbery."

Detective Littleton was not surprised. "Just like we thought it was. I'll let you know as soon as I get those phone records."

The following day, Detective Littleton received J. W. Walters's records and confirmed that he'd been in contact with Pete Johnson on an ongoing basis for months. In addition to the phone records, the investigators had secured J. W. Walters's handguns and shotgun. They also had Pete Johnson's cell phone and handgun. And now the detectives were ready to resume their conversation with J. W. Walters. And since they'd confirmed heroin possession as a component of the case, they invited Detective Mitchell and ADA Sanchez.

This formidable law enforcement team meant business. Walters had a court-appointed attorney, George Green. Detective Littleton requested that J. W. Walters be placed in interrogation room one. J. W. Walters had been in jail three days and was in bad shape physically and mentally because of his heroin addiction.

Detective Littleton opened the questioning. "Mr. Walters, you told us that you shot Pete Johnson because he attempted to rob you. Is that correct?"

"Yes."

"Did you have a personal relationship with Pete Johnson prior to the day that you killed him?"

J. W. Walters was attempting to cover up facts. "No."

Detective Littleton continued to push for the truth. "That's strange because your phone records indicate that you and Pete Johnson have known each other for months. It is my responsibility to inform you that it is a crime to knowingly make false statements to law enforcement officials during an investigation. Why did you lie to us about your relationship with Pete Johnson?"

J. W. Walters couldn't take it anymore. His drug addiction had him suffering. "I'm trying to stay out of trouble."

"What kind of trouble?" Detective Littleton asked.

J. W. Walters confessed, "I mean trouble with drugs and murder, that kind of trouble. Pete came to my office to murder me because I owe him ten thousand dollars. He attempted to pull his gun and shoot me, but I was ready for him because he'd called me and told me he was coming to kill me, but I got him first. Folks, I'm sick. I need some dope to get well, and I need it right now. If you help me, I'll tell you everything you want to know. I need help."

ADA Sanchez took charge. "Let's get him to the hospital and get him some methadone. We'll continue our investigation when he's stable. I want two guards on this man at all times inside and outside his room. He's a high-priority witness."

A team of officers took J. W. Walters to the hospital as the law enforcement team continued their meeting.

ADA Sanchez continued, "It's obvious that Walters understands that he's in serious trouble, and he sounds like he's ready to work with us."

Detective Phillips joined in. "Yeah, we've got him right where we want him. And we also have Pete Johnson's cell phone. So if Johnson is supplying Walters with heroin, who's supplying Johnson?"

Detective Mitchell saw a potential break in his drug case. "That's a great question, Detective Phillips. We have a list of suspects, including phone numbers, and we may get a match on Johnson's phone."

ADA Sanchez wanted to take full advantage of all of the evidence. "With the increase in crime and drugs all over the city, this could be the break we've been looking for. I want to hit these bastards hard, and about Walters, if he's helpful, I might cut him some slack. But if he's not, I'll put him in jail for a long time."

Sanchez continued, "After you've completed the investigation on the phone records and cell phones, I want this same team to come back together, share all of the information, and then plan our continued questioning of Walters. I want everyone in this room to understand that we're a team and our goal is to reduce crime in this city. And in order to do that, we can't just react. We have to act. We've got to outsmart these criminals and hit them hard at every opportunity."

They adjourned the meeting. The following day DA Adam Winston had a meeting with ADA Sanchez.

"Sanchez, when we lost ADA Barbara Davis, we lost one of the best crime fighters in the state. I want you to know that since you stepped in, you've been doing a great job, but I want you to do more. I want the criminals in the city and state to know that if they even think about harming a law enforcement official, we're going to get them. No matter how long it takes, we'll get every one of them. I want the criminals to be afraid to commit a crime in our city. We've got the best detectives in the nation, and if we push them, they can catch every criminal in this city. And it's your job to push them."

ADA Sanchez immediately reconvened the law enforcement team in her conference room. "So what have we learned from Pete Johnson's phone records?"

Detective Mitchell shared data. "We have confirmed three matches so far. Pete Johnson has been in repeated contact with three suspected heroin dealers: Josh Smith, Vicky Swanson, and Peter Williams."

ADA Sanchez wanted all the facts. "Do we have wiretaps on their phones?"

Detective Mitchell responded, "Yes, we do have wiretaps on each one."

ADA Sanchez was pushing. "We've got Walters, who claims Johnson sells him heroin. And we now know that Johnson is connected to Smith, Swanson, and Williams in the heroin trade. How's Walters?"

Detective Phillips gave an update. "He's stable."

ADA Sanchez was ready to apply pressure. "I want him and his attorney back in here tomorrow, and I want to know everything he knows about the heroin trade in our city. I want to take these four individuals and use them to go after the big boys. I want us to build strong enough cases against these four people that it will force them to work for us."

Detective Mitchell shared information. "We know Peter Williams has done time and is presently on probation, but we don't want to move on these people prematurely and give them a chance to warn their bosses."

ADA Sanchez agreed with Detective Mitchell to an extent. "You're right. We don't want to move prematurely, but we do want to move. We'll talk to Walters tomorrow, but for now we need to look at everything we have on Smith, Swanson, and Williams and make plans to take them down."

Meanwhile on the east side of town, in the apartment of Josh Smith, he and Vicky Swanson were discussing Pete Johnson.

Vicky was wondering aloud, "Josh, has anybody heard from Pete?"

"I haven't. Hell, knowing Pete, he's probably trying to find some more junkies to exploit."

They both laughed, and suddenly Smith's phone rang. Peter Williams was on the other end.

"This is Peter. Somebody killed Pete."

Josh Smith was shocked. "What? Who did it?"

"I heard some junkie shot him with a shotgun. Y'all be careful out there. I'll call you about the pickup later."

Josh informed Vicky, "Peter said somebody shot Pete with a shotgun and he's dead."

Vicky thought Pete was his own worst enemy. "Pete always thought he was a gangster. We can sell dope without that crap. I got the college kids sowed up, and the last thing they want to do is bite the hand that feeds them."

Both laughed.

"Josh, did Peter say who's taking Pete's place?"

"He didn't say, but you know when it comes to dealing dope, anybody can be replaced. Since we have some time, let's check out the bedroom."

"I'm with that, and I got some coke. And everybody knows things go better with coke."

They both laughed as they entered the bedroom.

The next day, the law enforcement team continued to plan their strategy.

ADA Sanchez was ready to make a move. "I want to arrest these three people: Josh Smith, Vicky Swanson, and Peter Williams. I want to press them for information. Add Walters to the list, and that gives us four sources. Do we know where any of these people live?"

Detective Mitchell described his information. "We know Vicky Swanson has an apartment on the east side of the city. And we've spotted her in restaurants spending a lot of time with college students. We know that heroin is all over the college campuses."

ADA Sanchez indicated that it was time to make an arrest, "Vicky Swanson is our highest-priority target, and I want her arrested right now."

Detective Mitchell explained, "We've made several buys from some of these college dealers, and we're in position to arrest them. We'll talk to J. W. Walters first. Then we'll make our move at the college."

"Great, let's do it." ADA Sanchez wanted results. She was pushing the action, and the detectives were responding.

On Thursday morning, the law enforcement team was meeting with J. W. Walters and his attorney. ADA Sanchez was in court, so Detective Mitchell opened the questioning.

"At our last meeting, you said Pete Johnson supplied you with heroin. Do you have any idea where he got his heroin?"

J. W.'s attorney, George Green, worked for a deal for his client. "My client needs to know what he can expect for his cooperation."

Detective Mitchell explained to J. W. Walters, "If we're able to lock up some bad guys with the information you give us, you can expect to keep your business and stay out of prison."

Green said, "I want the agreement in writing."

Detective Mitchell pushed the process along. "ADA Sanchez will get that to you. Now let's talk about heroin. But before you start, you need to know that if you lie to us one time, that cancels the chance for any deal."

J. W. Walters started to tell what he knew. "Pete Johnson used to talk about a guy named Peter. He said Peter had the best dope, he always had dope, and he was connected directly to the farm."

Detective Mitchell pressed Walters for more. "Where is the farm, and what kind of farm are we talking about?"

Walters didn't have all the answers. "I don't know. He just said there's always plenty of dope at the farm."

The team had Walters moved back to his cell, and they joined with the drug task force for a major operation, the college campus bust. The drug task force was made up of the FBI, state, county, and city law enforcement, including the members of the law enforcement team, and they had three no-knock warrants for three campus apartments. They executed them at approximately 11:00 p.m.

Bam! Bam! Bam!

The doors at three apartments flew open, and officers in protective gear with weapons drawn rushed into each apartment. Drug enforcement officers caught the students by complete surprise.

"Put your hands above your heads. Get your hands up!"

They quickly handcuffed and arrested six students, four men and two women. The prisoner's names were Freddie Hatfield, Don Murphy, Linda Ward, Brenda Hair, Billy Oaks, and Donald Scottsdale. They had 112,000 pills in their possession, including OxyContin, Percocet, and fentanyl, and ten pounds of heroin.

Detective Mitchell read them their rights. "You are being arrested for drug trafficking. You have the right to remain silent. Anything you say will be used against you in a court of law. You have the right to an attorney. If you cannot afford one, an attorney will be appointed to you. Do you understand the rights that I've just read to you?"

The prisoners all said yes, and they were put in police cars and taken to jail. They would be in jail over the weekend and have a bail hearing Monday morning. The next day, the news of the Thursday night campus drug bust was all over the morning news, and Vicky Swanson was petrified with fear. She'd had a lot of success using college students to sell drugs, but now her operation had fallen apart, and there were six witnesses ready to testify against her to avoid prison. Vicky didn't know what to do so she called the man she'd been sleeping with, Josh.

The phone rang and rang, but no one answered.

"Pick up the got-damn phone, Josh!"

She called and called, but Josh did not answer his phone. He knew it was her, but he also knew that if law enforcement were targeting her college drug dealers, so was she. That's the way it is in the drug business. When you're making money for the bosses and not making trouble, they love you, but if you make any trouble, they hate you. And at this moment, they hated Vicky Swanson.

She was extremely worried, and she had every right to be. Not only did she owe the drug bosses money, she was also a threat to their operation. She was considering her options. Should she try to get out of town, or should she go to the police? Whatever she did, she'd better do it in a hurry.

So she made a call. "Hello. Is this the police?"

"Yes, this is the police. Detective Bobby Mitchell speaking. What can I do for you?"

"This is Vicky Swanson, and I'm in big trouble. These drug dealers are going to try to kill me because of that drug bust last night. I need help! I want to turn myself in!"

Detective Mitchell was surprised to get a call from their main suspect, and he didn't want her to get away.

"Where are you?"

Vicky Swanson was about to panic. "I'm at the East Side Apartments, number forty-seven on Thirty-second and Fleetwood Street. Please hurry!"

Detective Mitchell attempted to relax her. "Don't worry. I'll send a car over to pick you up."

But before Detective Mitchell could hang up his phone, he heard the murder take place. Someone kicked in Vicky Swanson's door and opened fire,

Bam!

"Oh no! Don't kill me!"

Pop, pop, pop, pop, pop, pop, pop, pop, pop!

Detective Mitchell hung up the phone and called dispatch. "I need all cars in the vicinity of East Side Apartments, apartment number forty-seven at Thirty-second Street and Fleetwood, to get to that address right away. Vicky Swanson is a witness, and she's in danger. Shots have been fired."

Dispatch repeated his instructions, but when the officers arrived, it was too late. Someone had kicked the door in and shot Vicky Swanson six times. She was dead.

The police officer at the scene reported, "This is car one thirty-eight. We are at East Side Apartments, number forty-seven, and this is a crime scene. The door has been kicked in, and there is a female who appears to be deceased from multiple gunshots."

Shortly thereafter, Detectives Phillips, Corns, and Mitchell as well as the coroner and several additional officers were at the apartment of Vicky Swanson. They all agreed that this was a mob-style murder.

The killing affected Detective Mitchell. "They didn't want her talking so they killed her. She called my office for help, and I was on the phone with her when the murder took place. I heard everything."

Detective Phillips kept his eyes on the mission. "We still got other assets, Mitchell. We'll get the murdering drug dealers. What happened today is just that drug life. When do you plan on talking to Sanchez?"

Detective Mitchell attempted to refocus. "I better go see her right now."

Detective Phillips saw that Mitchell was impacted by what he heard. "Bobby, go talk to Sanchez. We'll take care of this crime scene, and I'll get you a copy of the report later."

Detective Mitchell called ADA Sanchez to schedule a meeting. "This is Narcotics Lead Detective Bobby Mitchell. Vicky Swanson was murdered at her apartment about an hour ago. I'm headed to your office to give you a briefing."

ADA Sanchez was disappointed. "I look forward to our discussion." Detective Mitchell got in his vehicle and headed to her office.

"Come on in and have a seat, Detective. So Vicky Swanson is dead?"

Detective Mitchell was still struggling with what he'd just experienced. "Yes, she is. She was shot six times. Thursday night's drug bust spooked the bosses, and she was trying to turn herself in, but she ran out of time."

ADA Sanchez was focused on the mission. "In less than twenty-four hours, these drug dealers reacted to our drug bust. Damn, these are some extremely dangerous people."

Detective Mitchell was still trying to cope. "I was on the phone with Swanson when they kicked the door in and shot her. It was automatic weapon fire. I thought I was a pretty tough guy, but hearing that homicide shook me up."

ADA Sanchez admonished the detective. "Detective, I suggest that you get unshook up because this fight is just getting started. If you haven't written your report, go ahead and do that now. I'm going to schedule a law enforcement team meeting for this afternoon. You'll get the email." Sanchez sent an email, scheduling a meeting for 2:00 p.m.

ADA Sanchez opened the team meeting. "Where are we with the Swanson killing?"

Detective Mitchell was regaining his focus. "Like I said previously, narcotics personnel had observed Vicky Swanson spending a lot of time with the college students that we busted last night. We believe that she was their drug supplier. We also believe her murder was in response to our busting and arresting those college students. She told me just before she was shot that some drug dealers were going to try to kill her because of Thursday night's bust. I was in the process of arranging her surrender over the phone when I heard the murder take place."

ADA Sanchez kept the focus moving forward. "Do you see how quickly these guys responded? In less than twenty-four hours, they're eliminating witnesses. And the only reason those college students are alive is because we've got them in jail. We have a bail hearing with those six students Monday morning. I want to be interrogating them no later than Monday afternoon. They'll have their parents and lawyers here so we'll be able to go at them. What has J. W. Walters given us?"

Detective Mitchell added, "According to Mr. Walters, we all heard him say that Pete Johnson was his heroin supplier. According to Walters, Pete Johnson, the man he killed, used to talk about a guy named Peter. He said Peter had the best dope and he always had dope because he was connected directly to the farm. We believe this Peter he's referring to is Peter Williams. My constructive speculation is that if we can locate Peter Williams and identify the location of this farm, we'll find a lot of drugs."

Detective Phillips was focused on the upcoming battle. "And they'll have a lot of guns. With the amount of drugs that we got off that college campus and considering the immediate subsequent related homicide, you can believe that these drug dealers will be ready for war. So we better be ready."

ADA Sanchez was ready for the fight. "That's a very good point, Detective Phillips. Based on our evidence, we're going after the big boys, and we damn sure better be ready. Determining the location of this farm is our next big deal. These college students might be able to help us with that. Peter Williams and Josh Smith should be able to help us with that also. It sounds like we've got enough telephonic data to connect them to Vicky Swanson. Maybe they were supplying her and she was supplying the college kids. Let's build a case against those bastards. Getting information from those college kids is our second-highest priority, with the farm being our number-one main concern. We have a big Monday coming. I plan to deny the students bail, and I plan to walk them from the courthouse to interrogation rooms one, two, and three. They'll be in pairs of twos, just like their living arrangements. And we'll go to work on them and find out more about this farm."

Detective Mitchell explained his plan. "We're just going to continue to monitor Peter Williams and Josh Smith and work toward building a case against them."

ADA Sanchez concurred. "That's correct, but as soon as we have adequate probable cause, I want those men in our possession. They could have murdered Vicky Swanson. If not, you better believe they know who did. If there's nothing else, let's go have a good weekend."

On Monday morning at 9:00 a.m., ADA Sanchez was in the courthouse for the bail hearing that was being heard by Judge Shirley Alexander. Each student had his or her parents and attorneys present. The students pleaded not guilty; each attorney requested bail since it was their first offense.

Judge Alexander called on ADA Sanchez. "ADA Sanchez, what's your response to the request for bail?"

ADA Sanchez was ready. "Judge Alexander, at the time of their arrest, these defendants had in their campus apartments 112,000 opiate pills, including OxyContin, Percocet, and fentanyl. They also had in their campus apartments ten pounds of pure heroin. Based on the police reports, these individuals had been selling these drugs to the student population at our local colleges for months, if not longer. Based on the quantity in their possession, they had no plans of quitting anytime soon. As a result of their drug trafficking, the number of drug-related deaths on our colleges campuses and throughout our city have increased. As a result of the obvious drug addictions that have resulted from their trafficking, crime has increased on our college campuses and in our city. These defendants are a part of a drug trafficking enterprise that is a present and increasing threat to every student and faculty member at our colleges, and they're a threat to every citizen of our city. As a result, I'm requesting that you deny bail for all defendants."

After listening to ADA Sanchez, Judge Alexander made her ruling. "Bail is denied. And I'm scheduling the trial date for a month from today's date. It will begin at nine in the morning here in this courtroom."

Police officers escorted the students back to their jail cells. At 10:00 a.m., the students were escorted from their cells to interrogation rooms one, two, and three. During the interrogation of one of the prisoners, Linda Ward, Detective Mitchell asked if she'd ever heard of or visited the farm. He was pursuing the law enforcement team's primary target.

Joe L. Growth, Linda Ward's attorney, spoke on behalf of his client. "Before my client provides any response, how is this going to help her?"

Detective Mitchell pushed forward. "You know how this process works. If her input leads to arrest and convictions, it will help toward a reduced sentence. Let me call the assistant district attorney."

Detective Mitchell called ADA Sanchez and explained the situation. "This is Detective Mitchell. I've got a lawyer here wanting to know what his client gets for her testimony. Can you come to interrogation room one?"

"I'm on the way."

At 10:45 a.m., she arrived at interrogation room one and went to work. "Look, the quality of your information is what will help you, and the sooner you get the information to us carries a lot of weight as well. You're presently facing twenty to twenty-five years in prison, and I'm the one that's going to be prosecuting you. Help us catch some bad guys, and I can cut your sentence in half. I'll be straight with you. I'm not in the mood to play games. Your contact, Vicky Swanson, was murdered last Friday morning. We believe whoever was supplying her drugs for you college students are the ones who killed her. We also believe that if you were not in jail, they would have killed you too."

Joe Growth instructed his client, "Answer their questions, Linda."

"I was sleeping with Josh Smith, but Vicky didn't know because she was sleeping with him too. Sometimes Josh would brag about their drug operation. He said no one would ever suspect a hay farm as one of the largest drug operations in the state."

ADA Sanchez pushed for answers. "Did he ever say where the hay farm is located?"

Linda knew she was in big trouble and started to cry. "He never told me that."

ADA Sanchez ordered all of the students taken back to their jail cells. She called her secretary and requested her to contact all members of the law enforcement team to be ready to meet in her conference room in fifteen minutes.

ADA Sanchez met with the team and pursued the target. "We just had one of the students tell us that these drug dealers are using a hay farm as a cover for their drug operation, That lines up with what J. W. Walters had told us previously. Does anyone know how many hay farms we have near the city?"

Detective Mitchell decided to bring in help. "I'll contact the sheriff department and my contact with the drug task force and bring them up to speed." He left the room.

ADA Sanchez continued, "Josh Smith is our hottest target because he has specific details on the hay farm operation. I want him in our possession before the drug bosses get a chance to murder him. Detective Phillips, how is the Vicky Swanson murder case progressing?"

Detective Phillips was ready. "I've had people reviewing security camera footage from the East Side apartment complex. We've discovered that two men wearing ski masks got out of a Chevrolet pickup truck. They are responsible for the break-in and murder. There were no tags on the truck. We've got people watching the last known addresses of Peter Williams and Josh Smith."

ADA Sanchez wanted action and results. "Has anyone called the phone number that we have for Josh Smith to tell that fool that he's going to be killed if he doesn't turn himself in?"

Detective Phillips responded, "We've been calling that number, but we haven't gotten a response so far."

ADA Sanchez pressed on. "We got the hay farm tip from one of the college student drug dealers by the name of Linda Ward. She and Josh Smith were bed buddies."

Detective Phillips got a call and stepped out of the room. Sergeant Vance Franklyn had good news.

"A man by the name of Josh Smith just turned himself in. He's presently under guard in interrogation room one."

Detective Phillips was pleased with the news. "Please have him brought to the assistant district attorney's conference room. Thank you."

Detective Phillips reentered the conference room. "We just got a big break. Josh Smith just turned himself in, and they're bringing him here at this very moment."

At 12:15 p.m., two officers escorted Josh Smith into the conference room and sat him down. The officers exited the room and waited in the corridor.

ADA Sanchez took the lead. "Where's the hay farm located? We don't have time to fuck around. Two people are already dead."

Josh Smith started to talk. "I know two people are already dead. I loved Vicky, and that's why I'm here. The farm is located about five miles west of the city, and it's heavily armed. They've got tons of pills and heroin. It's a major distribution point in the state. It's the Breaks Hay Farm."

ADA Sanchez called her secretary, Mary Douglas. "Mary, it's Maria. Contact the commander of the drug task force and tell him to call me and make plans to meet with me today. Tell him it's bigger than the college bust. I also need you to contact Judge Alexander and tell her that I need a drug warrant for Breaks Hay Farm. The probable cause is eyewitness testimony of Josh Smith, Linda Ward, and J. W. Walters. Thank you very much." ADA Sanchez was wasting no time making plans to hit the drug dealers hard.

At 1:30 p.m., her phone rang. The commander of the drug task force, William Bell, was on the line.

"This is Commander Bell. I got your message, and I'm ready to respond."

"I've got three witnesses that tell me that the Breaks Hay Farm is a massive opiate pills and heroin distribution operation. That farm was supplying the college dealers. I've requested a warrant, and we need to organize the execution of this warrant as soon as possible because the college bust tipped them off and they're killing witnesses."

At approximately 4:30 p.m., there were 350 law enforcement officials representing the drug task force, including FBI, state, county, city law enforcement, and the law enforcement team. They closed the entrance to the Breaks Hay Farm. The hay farm consisted of 180 acres, and the majority of the space was hay field. But it also had five large barns with basements, a fueling station for eighteen-wheelers, an office complex, and a main house. There were tractors, hay-gathering equipment, and several eighteen-wheelers, but some of the trucks were not the type used for hauling hay.

When the drug task force arrived, some of the eighteen-wheelers were being loaded as if they planned to leave right away, but were caught off guard by the sudden arrival of law enforcement. The occupants, approximately two hundred people of the farm, were well armed. They had M60 machine guns, .50-caliber machine guns, AR-15s, and all types of handguns. But the drug task force was well armed also. Plus they had air support with tear gas.

Commander Bell used a loudspeaker. "This is the drug task force. We have a warrant to search the entire property listed under the name of Breaks Hay Farm, including any and all personnel, buildings, equipment, and/or grounds. We're requesting that all personnel that are presently at this location walk toward the entrance in a single line with hands raised above your heads. Do not attempt to put your hands in your pockets, and do not attempt to carry anything with you. Do not attempt to make any phone calls. Do not attempt to drive any vehicles. And please provide personal identification to the officers as you walk past."

The commander got no response. "For the second time, I'm asking you to."

Gunfire from the drug dealers interrupted him.

Pop, pop, pop, pop, pop, pop, pop, pop, pop, pop, pop, pop, pop, pop, pop, pop, pop, pop, pop, pop, pop!

The officers returned fire.

Pop, pop, pop, pop, pop, pop, pop, pop, pop, pop, pop, pop, pop, pop, pop, pop, pop, pop, pop, pop, pop!

Commander Bell ordered air support. "Bring the air support in, and drop that tear gas right on top of them. I want you to hit them with everything you got!"

The hay farm became a war zone.

Boom! Boom! Boom! Boom! Boom! Boom!

Pop, pop, pop, pop, pop, pop, pop, pop, pop, pop, pop, pop, pop, pop, pop, pop, pop, pop!

Boom! Boom! Boom! Boom! Boom! Boom!

Pop, pop, pop, pop, pop, pop, pop, pop, pop, pop, pop, pop, pop, pop, pop, pop!

Machine gun fire hit one of the helicopters. It crashed into a barn and exploded. Kaboom! The barn was on fire. Yet the gunfight continued.

Pop, pop!

Boom! Boom! Boom! Boom! Boom! Boom!

Pop, pop, pop, pop, pop, pop, pop, pop, pop, pop, pop, pop, pop, pop, pop, pop!

Boom! Boom! Boom! Boom! Boom! Boom!

Suddenly someone from the office complex window was waving a broom handle with a white dress shirt tied to it. The drug dealers had had enough.

Commander Bell used the loudspeaker to order a cease fire. "Cease fire! You drug dealers put down your weapons. Put both of your hands on the top of your head and walk toward the entrance in a single line."

A drug dealer yelled from a window, "We need medical attention in here!"

Commander Bell responded, "The injured will get medical attention when those of you who can walk come out here and turn yourselves in to law enforcement personnel. So do as you've been told: put your hands on your head and walk in a single line toward the entrance now!"

It had gotten dark outside, and law enforcement had set up additional exterior lighting to closely monitor the surrender. Each drug dealer that was able followed instructions and was handcuffed and put on a bus. There were 123 drug dealers arrested, 36 wounded, and 44 killed. Some of the prisoners were read their rights on the bus; others were read their rights at the hospital.

At 10:30 p.m., law enforcement had complete control of the Breaks Hay Farm. They had lost twenty-one officers, and thirty-three were wounded. They discovered tons of heroin and opiate pills on the trucks and in the barn's basements.

The following day ADA Sanchez was at her desk, thinking over the previous day's success, when DA Adam Winston dropped by unannounced.

"Good morning, ADA Sanchez."

"Good morning, DA Winston."

DA Winston was very pleased with ADA Sanchez's leadership. "I wanted to come by and thank you personally for the fine work that the law enforcement team under your leadership accomplished yesterday. It would have made the late ADA Davis very proud. You are the best that we have, and it's an honor and a pleasure working with you. Keep up the great work that you're doing and have a good day."

"Thank you." ADA Sanchez appreciated every word her boss had said, but she was so tired from yesterday's events that all she could do was enjoy a bottle of water. She asked her secretary to schedule a law enforcement team meeting for 2:00 p.m. today.

She got a phone call from Detective Phillips. "This is Detective Phillips. How are you today? I just wanted you to know that I think you're doing a hell of a job. When's the next meeting?"

ADA Sanchez appreciated the support. "I'm doing great, and thank you. It's all about teamwork. The meeting is at two o'clock in my conference room today."

Detective Phillips was looking forward to the meeting. "I'll see you at two."

ADA Sanchez convened the law enforcement team meeting. "Congratulations on yesterday's work. We got a lot of drugs off the street. We still don't know who the owner of Breaks Hay Farm is, but we've got a hundred and fifty prisoners who are all facing the death penalty or life in prison. So I'm sure we'll get the owner soon."

Detective Phillips offered input. "He's probably trying to get out of the country or talking to his politician friends for help."

ADA Sanchez continued to push. "I want him in our jail right now. He's our number-one target."

Detective Mitchell offered an opinion. "With this size operation, there's no telling who's on the take."

Detective Littleton focused on the owner. "The owner is hoping that we're so busy processing the drugs and criminals that we take our eyes off him."

ADA Sanchez agreed with Detective Littleton. "That's a very good point, and that's why it's important to stay focused on the owner. I'll pursue the name, but in case I'm blocked, you guys pursue it as well. Pressure the criminals to help us identify who owns that farm. And remember, keep your eyes open for anyone trying to redirect our effort from the owner to someone else. We've got a drug task force meeting tomorrow at ten, and I need all you guys to be there. The meeting will be in the main conference room in DA Winston's office suite. I've also got to get ready for a bail hearing for a hundred and fifty-six people."

"That's a lot of people. How do you plan to handle it?" Detective Littleton asked.

"I'll just treat the group like they're one person since they're all part of a drug-dealing enterprise and took part in the killing of law enforcement officers. I'm recommending no bail for any of them."

They all laughed as they ended the meeting.

It was the day of the bail hearing for Breaks Hay Farm prisoners.

Judge Alexander questioned the defense, "How do you plead?"

The attorney for Breaks Hay Farm responded, "We plead not guilty."

Judge Alexander wanted to hear from the assistant district attorney. "ADA Sanchez, what's your response?"

Confidence filled ADA Sanchez. "Judge, all of these people are part of a drug trafficking enterprise that caused the death of twenty-one law enforcement officers, and they wounded another twenty-three officers who were all attempting to carry out their official duties. Breaks Hay Farm itself was used as a cover to conceal this criminal enterprise. This hay farm also supplied opiate pills and heroin to our college drug dealers, whom we recently arrested. Once law enforcement got control of the farm, after these defendants had shot at them for several hours, they discovered tons of opiate pills and heroin. These people are a clear danger to the taxpaying citizens of this city and state. I'm requesting that you deny bail."

Judge Alexander concurred. "Bail is denied. I'm setting the trial date for two months from today's date."

ADA Sanchez got out of court just in time for the drug task force meeting. There were officials from the FBI, state, county, city, and law enforcement team present.

DA Winston opened the meeting. "I just wanted to start the meeting by saying job well done. And now I want to turn this over to the person who has been spearheading the law enforcement team who secured critical evidence and made yesterday's success possible, ADA Maria Sanchez."

ADA Sanchez was surprised that she was going to be chairing the meeting because she had no advanced notice, but she was more than ready. "After doing some digging, I've discovered that the owner of the Breaks Hay Farm is Howard B. Sharks, and we've had a hard time locating him. Does anybody have any idea where this man is?"

FBI Agent Harold Holly provided some insight. "According to our investigators, he lives in Illinois, and we've been tracking his movement ever since his property came under suspicion."

ADA Sanchez wanted Mr. Shark arrested. "Someone with proper jurisdiction needs to arrest him and his wife right now and bring them here and put them in our jail."

Agent Holly made his move. "All we were waiting for was for someone in charge to give the order." He stepped out into the corridor, called the Illinois FBI office, and ordered the arrest of Mr. and Mrs. Howard B. Sharks immediately. And once arrested, they were to be transported to New Mexico. After the call, he stepped back into the meeting.

ADA Sanchez pressed forward. "These people brought between fifty and a hundred tons of heroin and pills into this state. Where did it come from? It originated somewhere, and we need to know where. Do any of you have ongoing drug cases that might relate to yesterday's bust? If you're generating reports, I need copies, and the sooner the better. This case is going to trial in two months, and I'm not in the mood for mercy. We need to press the prisoners for information and make it clear that I'm pursuing the death penalty. Our top priority is arresting Mr.

and Mrs. Howard B. Sharks and pressing them for information, but the second-highest concern is finding out where all these damn drugs are coming from. Let there be no doubt in anyone's mind that we're going after the big boys."

As Detectives Phillips and Littleton left the meeting, Phillips raised an interesting point. "That was a good meeting. Have you noticed the chief is keeping a very low profile these days? I haven't seen him in a single meeting."

Detective Littleton responded, "Hell, Phillips, he's getting ready to retire. I don't think he's been in a meeting in two years." They both laughed.

Detective Phillips changed the subject. "ADA Sanchez is doing a hell of a job. I think she's going to be the next DA, and I like working with her."

Detective Littleton agreed. "I know she's very hands-on. She wants to be out there where the bullets are flying."

They both laughed some more as they prepared to end the day and get some needed rest. Meanwhile, the Chicago FBI office had made plans to arrest Howard B. Sharks and his wife as they attempted to board a flight to Russia. The FBI approached Mr. and Mrs. Sharks when they were about to board the plane.

Agent Ben Huntsville made his move. "Mr. Shark, I'm Agent Ben Huntsville, and I have a warrant for your arrest."

At least six agents were with Agent Huntsville, and they secured the Sharks.

"You and your wife, Mrs. Hattie Sharks, are under arrest on the charges of drug trafficking and the death and wounding of multiple law enforcement officials at the Breaks Hay Farm. Put your hands behind your back because the law requires me to handcuff you both."

Mr. and Mrs. Sharks were handcuffed. Agent Huntsville read them their rights. "You have the right to remain silent, and anything you say will be used against you in a court of law. You have the right to an attorney. If you can't afford an attorney, one will be appointed to you. Do you understand the rights that I've just read to you?"

Mrs. Hattie Sharks was shocked and upset. "Yes, I understand! Now Howard, what the hell have you got us into? We're getting stopped at the airport like common criminals. You son of a bitch, I knew something was up when you got in a big hurry to go to Russia. I didn't want to go to Russia. No damn way! Howard, you bastard, answer me! I want to know what the hell is going on. You bastard, I've never been arrested in my life, and now at seventy-one years old, I get handcuffed in this damn airport like a common criminal. You tell me what you did, you bastard. I hate you. What the hell have you done to me?"

Agent Huntsville made a request. "Put them in separate cars."

ADA Sanchez received a call from the Chicago FBI office. "This is Agent Ben Huntsville with the Chicago FBI office. I wanted you to know that we've arrested Howard B. Sharks and his wife, Hattie Sharks. They were attempting to get on a flight to Russia at the time of the arrest. They should be in your office no later than one o'clock tomorrow."

ADA Sanchez was pleased with the news. "Thank you, Agent Huntsville. That will teach them to try to outrun the law. I can go home now and get a good night's sleep. I really love it when people do their job."

The following morning ADA Sanchez scheduled a law enforcement team meeting for 10:30 a.m. in the district attorney's conference room.

"First thing this morning we've got some great news. The Chicago FBI office arrested the owner of the Breaks Hay Farm, Howard B. Sharks, and his wife, Hattie Sharks, trying to get on a plane to Russia."

Detective Mitchell drew a conclusion. "Russia? That explains all of these drugs."

ADA Sanchez continued, "We've got to pressure these witnesses. Russia now becomes the suspected main supplier for the drugs. So unless another new and better target surfaces, Russians operating in this country are our targets. Right now the owners of that farm are facing the death penalty. They won't be getting any bail, so their freedom is gone. We need to find out who the head of operations at the hay farm is. We need to know where they pick this dope up and where they are loading these trucks. Out of all these people that we've arrested, we've got to get some good information. What else have we got?"

Detective Phillips reported, "The pickup truck that the killers drove to and from Vicky Swanson's apartment the day she was murdered has turned up at the Breaks Hay Farm. We're pulling fingerprints from the vehicle, and we plan to compare them with everyone we arrested at that farm, alive or dead, and I strongly suspect we'll be able to identify our murderers."

ADA Sanchez responded, "That's some great news, Phillips. Let's keep it going and keep applying pressure, and I'm convinced we're going to accomplish our goals. If there's nothing else, I've got to run home, but I should be back in an hour. See you later."

ADA Sanchez got in her vehicle and headed home to pick up some documents. She pulled up in her driveway, got out of her car, and approached her front door when a black 2008 Honda sped by and fired an automatic weapon.

Pop, pop, pop, pop, pop, pop, pop, pop, pop, pop!

A neighbor looked out her window as ADA Sanchez was shot three times in the head and neck and three times in her lower body. She was dead before she hit the ground. The neighbor called the police.

Police dispatch announced, "Shots fired at 77 Mulberry Lane. The victim is on the ground. All cars in that vicinity proceed to that address!"

Detective Phillips was talking with Detective Littleton in the corridor when the all-points bulletin was announced. He didn't know that the shooting was at ADA Sanchez's home.

"77 Mulberry Lane. That's a very upscale neighborhood. I wonder what the hell's going on."

A few moments later, an officer at the scene called in the shocking information. "This is car one eighty-seven, and we're at 77 Mulberry Lane. ADA Maria Sanchez is lying at her doorstep, and she's been shot several times and appears to be deceased."

Detectives Phillips and Littleton ran out of the door, got in a departmental vehicle, and drove to the address of the shooting. While on the way, they called for the homicide team, emergency services, medical examiner, coroner's office, and several officers.

Detectives Phillips and Littleton arrived at the home of ADA Sanchez and were shocked to see this once-energetic crime fighter lying motionless in the doorway of her home. Meanwhile, after hearing of the shooting of ADA Sanchez, DA Winston immediately called Agent Holly.

"I want to inform you that ADA Maria Sanchez has been shot and is believed to be deceased. We need to protect those prisoners, Harold B. Sharks and his wife, Hattie Sharks, that you are bringing in today at all costs. Your future contact on this issue is ADA Robert Jefferson."

Agent Holly responded, "We're scheduled to have those prisoners at your location today at one o'clock."

DA Winston immediately called ADA Jefferson. "ADA Jefferson, this is DA Winston. It's been reported that ADA Sanchez has been murdered, and you're the next man up. Her caseload now becomes yours, and I'll reassign your work. If you haven't been to the firing range lately, you may want to go. Please proceed to her home at 77 Mulberry Lane, which is where the shooting took place. The homicide team is already there. I suspect that this was a retaliation killing for the recent drug bust. Jefferson, this is a real drug war. The FBI is bringing in two prisoners from Chicago today at one o'clock. They own that hay farm that we busted. The FBI caught them getting on a plane to Russia."

ADA Jefferson responded, "I'm heading to the crime scene right now." He put on his shoulder holster and inserted his .45 automatic in the holster. He put on his jacket and headed out the door to his car and to the scene.

ADA Jefferson arrived at the home of ADA Sanchez and spoke with the detectives. "I'm Assistant District Attorney Robert Jefferson, and I'm replacing my late colleague, Maria Sanchez."

"I'm Homicide Detective Virgil Phillips."

ADA Jefferson sought out information. "What do we think happened?"

Detective Phillips explained, "It appears that someone was watching her or her home, maybe both. As soon as they got an opportunity, they did a drive-by shooting and hit her six times. We've been hitting these drug dealers hard over the last month. We've arrested over a hundred and fifty people. We've killed and wounded about eighty people, and we've confiscated a hundred tons of opiate pills and heroin. It appears that today they decided to hit back."

ADA Jefferson continued, "The law enforcement team has two prisoners, Howard B. Sharks and Hattie Sharks, coming in from Chicago at one o'clock. DA Winston will receive them. We'll meet them in interrogation room one. I'm headed back as soon as I get the call."

At that moment Jefferson's phone rang. "This is DA Winston. Those priority prisoners are here."

"I'm on the way."

The law enforcement team, with ADA Jefferson replacing the late ADA Sanchez, was meeting with the owners of the Breaks Hay Farm in separate rooms. Mrs. Hattie Sharks and her attorney, Franklyn M. Thomas, were in room one. Mr. Harold B. Sharks and his attorney, Hanley P. George, were in room two. The team decided to meet with Mrs. Sharks first.

ADA Jefferson opened the questioning. "Is it true that you are co-owner with your husband of the Breaks Hay Farm?"

Mrs. Hattie Sharks answered, "Yes, that's one of our properties."

"Are you aware that law enforcement officials seized that property three days ago?"

Mrs. Hattie Sharks hesitated and then answered, "No, I was not until today when my attorney informed me."

ADA Jefferson applied pressure. "Were you aware that your hay farm was being used as a major drug trafficking operation?"

Mrs. Hattie Sharks was getting more uncomfortable. "No, I was not."

ADA Jefferson wanted her to break. "Law enforcement officials confiscated between fifty to one hundred tons of opiate pills and heroin from your property. And there were seventeen law enforcement officials killed and another twenty-three injured during the seizure. That could get you and your husband life in prison or the death penalty, if we confirm that you profited from this drug operation."

Mrs. Hattie Sharks felt the pressure. "Life in prison or death penalty! I'm telling you I don't know anything about what's going on at that property. You'll have to talk to my husband about that."

ADA Jefferson kept the pressure on. "If your name is on the deed, you have some responsibility for what went on at that property. Is that property leased to anyone?"

Mrs. Hattie Sharks started to shake with fear. "You'll have to ask my husband about that."

ADA Jefferson continued to press her. "You've never seen and you have no knowledge of a lease agreement for the Breaks Hay Farm? And before you answer, it is my duty to inform you that it is a crime to make false statements to a law enforcement official during an investigation. And if it is proven that you knowingly made false or misleading statements to me or any other officials involved in this investigation, you will go to prison for an additional five years. So I'm going to ask you again: is the Breaks Hay Farm leased to anyone presently, or has it ever been leased to anyone?"

Franklyn Thomas intervened. "My client must have some consideration for her assistance."

ADA Jefferson continued, "Mr. Thomas, this is a capital murder and drug trafficking case, and your client has already given one misleading answer. If I were you, I would advise her to answer each question as truthfully as possible because any other answer would bring serious consequences. Now, I want to know if that property is leased to anyone."

Mrs. Hattie Sharks answered, "It was leased to a man named Barney Henderson."

"Where can I locate him? And don't delay me," ADA Jefferson warned.

"His name is Barney Henderson, and he has a cocktail lounge on 110th Street. 110th Street Lounge."

ADA Jefferson had all he needed to make the arrest. "Detectives, go arrest Barney Henderson and shut down his lounge. Tell those officers to take Mr. and Mrs. Sharks back to their cells, and make sure they don't talk."

ADA Jefferson called his office and requested that they secure a no-knock arrest warrant for Barney Henderson, related to the Breaks Hay Farm case. The probable cause was testimony of property owner Hattie Sharks. The warrant was secured.

Later that day, the law enforcement team arrived at the 110th Street Lounge, and officers covered every exit. The detectives and twenty officers, all wearing protective gear, entered through the front door with weapons drawn.

Detective Phillips took charge. "Everyone put your hands in the air and don't make a move!" He approached the bartender. "Where is Barney Henderson?"

"He's in his office."

"Lead us to it. Let's go!" Detective Phillips ordered.

When law enforcement arrived at Henderson's office door, they opened it and rushed in.

Detective Phillips gave Henderson a command. "Hang up the phone and stand up. Put the handcuffs on him. Barney Henderson, you are under arrest for capital murder and drug trafficking. You have the right to remain silent. Anything you say will be used against you. You have the right to an attorney. If you cannot afford an attorney, an attorney will be appointed to you. Do you understand the rights that I've just read to you?"

Barney Henderson was shocked but able to speak. "Yes, I do understand."

Police officers escorted Barney Henderson to a police car, put him in the back seat, and carried him to jail. Detective Phillips told everyone in the lounge that it was closed and everyone had to leave.

Meanwhile, back at his office, ADA Jefferson called Hattie Sharks' attorney, Franklyn M. Thomas. "This is ADA Robert Jefferson. Tell your client if she provides us a copy of that lease, it will help her. And we need it right now."

The attorney tried to help his client. "I'll tell her. If she has it and gives it to you, can she get bail?"

ADA Jefferson responded, "The more she helps, the better her chances."

The lawyer pushed for leniency. "You know her husband is the real criminal."

ADA Jefferson was not in a mood for mercy. "She should have divorced him."

The following day, ADA Jefferson secured the proper warrants and had expert investigators search the lounge from top to bottom. They found a copy of the lease agreement between Barney Henderson and Howard and Hattie Sharks. It had been expired for a week.

ADA Jefferson contacted the jail administrator to have Barney Henderson brought to interrogation room one at 9:00 a.m. He also emailed the members of the law enforcement team about the nine o'clock meeting. When the officers arrived with Barney Henderson at interrogation room one, the law enforcement team was there waiting for him.

ADA Jefferson opened the questioning. "Where did you get a hundred tons of heroin and pills?"

Attorney Lenny F. Williams was representing Barney Henderson. "What does my client get for helping you?"

ADA Jefferson had no patience for bargaining with a murderer. "He might get to live, but he needs to start talking right now."

The attorney was trying to save his client's life. "He wants the death penalty off the table, and he wants protective custody."

ADA Jefferson left the door open for protective custody. "If you can show us where the drugs are coming from and how they're shipped from state to state and country to country as well as how they're loaded and unloaded and where they originate. If you can do that, I'm certain we can let you live and protect you. But you need to start talking right now!"

With a nod from his attorney, Barney Henderson started talking. "I can show you how thousands of tons of drugs are shipped into this country every day."

ADA Jefferson walked to the door, opened it, and asked the two officers waiting in the corridor to move the prisoner and his attorney into the corridor for a few minutes. ADA Jefferson wanted to have a private discussion with the team to make sure they were in agreement.

"I wanted to make sure that we're all on the same page about taking the death penalty off the table and granting protective custody for this guy."

Detective Mitchell wanted to make the deal. "This guy's testimony gives us an opportunity to take down an international drug trafficking organization. That kind of opportunity does not happen often. What do you think, Phillips?"

"It makes sense to use this guy and take down as many criminals as we can. I think that's the greatest tribute we can pay to our fallen colleagues. What do you think, Littleton?"

"Catching hundreds of criminals and confiscating thousands of tons of drugs means we're doing our jobs at the highest level. I'm for it."

Detective Phillips alerted the team, "This drug war is going heat up big time, and there's going to be some major retaliation. It's my job as a homicide expert to point this out. So we got to stay ready, and we've got to make sure all of our people are ready."

ADA Jefferson asked the officers to bring the prisoner and his attorney back into the room. ADA Jefferson confirmed the agreement. "The death penalty is off the table, and you'll get protection if we get convictions. Listen, Henderson, we want to know it all, so when you start talking, don't stop until you tell us everything you know. You need to understand that one lie can kill your deal."

Barney Henderson started talking. "This is a Russian operation, and a lot of Americans who are addicted to greed are helping them. They have a trucking company, Large International Trucking, Inc. It's located on the northeast end of the city. It's a cover for another major heroin and opiate distribution operation, just like the hay farm. They ship and receive drugs from there, day and night. They've got more guns than they had at the hay farm."

ADA Jefferson contacted the jail administrator to arrange for Barney Henderson's protective custody. He also ordered four officers to escort Mr. Henderson to the office of jail administration and turn him over to the protective custody staff.

ADA Jefferson planned the next strike. "Now that we have this out of the way, let's plan our next step. We've got to take Large International

Trucking, Inc. down, and we've got to move fast. They know they're next with the college and the hay farm bust, and if they don't know that, they are really naïve. Detective Mitchell, we need your team to start surveillance on that trucking company. Please proceed with that, and you'll be getting a group email on the next drug task force meeting. Starting right now, you are our eyes and ears on that company."

Detective Mitchell pulled out his cell as he was leaving the room. Also ADA Jefferson called and instructed his secretary to schedule a drug task force meeting for 1:00 p.m. today in the district attorney's conference room. And he instructed her to contact Judge Alexander for a drug warrant for Large International Trucking, Inc. The probable cause was high-level informants employed by the drug enterprise. The primary probable cause informant was Barney Henderson. This was connected to the college and Breaks Hay Farm Enterprise.

ADA Jefferson was ready to go. "We've got to hit today."

Detective Littleton made a recommendation. "We've also got to make prisoner housing a top priority because if we don't, we're going to have a big problem. I recommend that we add Dianne Jackson, our jail administrator, to the law enforcement team because that keeps her in the loop. And it gives her advanced notice and helps avoid a housing crisis."

ADA Jefferson concurred. "Great idea, Detective Littleton. Would you make contact with her and invite her to the one o'clock meeting? Please proceed with that."

Detective Phillips got a phone call. While he took his call, ADA Jefferson left the room with cell phone in hand, headed back to his office. He gave Phillips a thumbs-up as he was walking out the door.

Detective Phillips continued with his call. "This is Detective Corns, and we've got a fingerprint match off that truck in the Vicky Swanson murder. It's a guy we've already arrested at the hay farm bust."

Detective Phillips responded, "That's great news, Corns. Proceed with our standard operating procedure. We've got a drug task force meeting today at one and a drug bust probably at four or five. It's a big target, bigger than the hay farm. So get our personnel ready. The narcotics team already has an eye on the target. I'll keep you informed as the strategy develops. Tell our people good job on that Swanson murder. You guys keep up the good work."

After getting back to his office, ADA Jefferson called the local FBI. "This is ADA Robert Jefferson. I've been assigned the late ADA Maria Sanchez's cases."

Agent Holly responded, "Yes, DA Winston informed me that you are now my point of contact."

ADA Jefferson continued, "We've identified another heroin and opiate large-scale distribution center. The narcotics team has an eye on them, and they'll have a report at the one o'clock drug task force meeting. The target is Large International Trucking, Inc."

Agent Holly responded, "Yeah, I got an email from your staff about the meeting. We appreciate the timely notice. We'll be there, prepared to go to work."

Jefferson had a plea hearing with Judge Alexander, and he headed to the courtroom.

Judge Alexander opened the hearing. "ADA Robert Jefferson, I understand that both sides have reached an agreement."

"Yes, Judge, all six defendants have pleaded guilty to first-offense drug trafficking and will serve a mandatory eight years of a twenty-five year sentence, with seven years of probation. If they violate that probation, they'll serve the full twenty-five years."

Judge Alexander kept the hearing moving. "Thank you, ADA Jefferson. Do you have any questions for these prisoners?"

"No, Judge, I do not."

Judge Alexander turned her attention to the defendants. "As for you six young people in front of me today, you had a good life. You've got good parents, you were attending a good college, and you had an opportunity for a good future. But because of the bad decisions that you made, you have interrupted your life, and it's going to be replaced with some very challenging times. For you and your family's sake, I hope you make better decisions in the future. Take them away."

ADA Jefferson got a call from Detective Littleton, who was with the new member of the team. "ADA Jefferson, Dianne Jackson and I are in my office."

"I'll be there in five minutes." ADA Jefferson headed to Detective Littleton's office. He entered and took a seat.

"Assistant District Attorney Robert Jefferson, this is jail administrator Dianne Jackson."

"It's good to meet you, Ms. Jackson."

"It's good to meet you, ADA Jefferson."

ADA Jefferson stayed focused. "As you are very well aware, recently we've been locking up a lot of criminals, and some of those are informants that we need to protect. At the time, Barney Henderson is our top-priority informant."

Dianne Jackson responded, "We presently have Barney Henderson isolated and secured. We also have standard operating procedures for priority inmates, so I don't see any problem housing your priority prisoners. We also have backup plans for a large influx of prisoners, and actually with the increase in heroin, crack, meth, cocaine, and pills, we are routinely operating under our emergency housing circumstances. Let me add that I appreciate this discussion because the more up-front information we can get, the better we can do our part."

ADA Jefferson continued, "Did Detective Littleton mention that I want you to serve as a permanent member of our law enforcement team?"

Detective Littleton interjected, "No, I didn't mention that to Ms. Jackson because I thought that should come from you."

ADA Jefferson explained, "Well, Ms. Jackson, Detective Littleton recommended making prisoner housing a permanent part of the law enforcement team since housing criminals is just as important as catching criminals. That's why I want you to work with us on a permanent basis, and I hope you will accept the appointment."

"As I said earlier, to be in a position to get housing requirement information as early in the process as possible is a real asset, and so with that in mind, I do accept the appointment."

ADA Jefferson was pleased with her response. "Thank you for accepting the appointment, and to show my appreciation, I invite you to our one o'clock drug task force meeting."

They all laughed and headed to the meeting. ADA Jefferson opened the meeting.

"The first thing I want to do is introduce a new member to the law enforcement team, and as such, she is also a member of the drug task force, Ms. Dianne Jackson, our jail administrator. I also need to introduce myself to some of you. I'm ADA Jefferson, and I was assigned the cases of our colleague, the late ADA Sanchez, whom we lost in the line of duty fighting this drug war. Our target today is the Large International Trucking, Inc. It is a drug distribution operation. Our narcotics division has been monitoring the activities at that location, and I'm going to ask Detective Mitchell to share what they observed."

"There are several large warehouses identical to the ones at the Breaks Hay Farm. There's a lot of unloading and loading of eighteen-wheelers at the warehouses. There are multiple fueling stations. There's a large office complex similar to the one at Breaks Hay Farm. There's more personnel standing guard, and all of their weapons are concealed. And there are fifteen to twenty eighteen-wheelers parked at the site, along with multiple cars and pickup trucks."

ADA Jefferson continued, "Thank you, Detective Mitchell. We're in for a fight, and I know we're ready. Look at the big screen, and you'll see there are two entryways. We want to close and control those immediately. You can also see that there's an abandoned mall in close proximity for our staging. I'm going to turn things over to the Commander Bell of the drug task force, and he will provide additional details."

"Thank you, ADA Jefferson. We're going to go about this bust in a similar manner that we went about the last one. We'll demand their surrender, and if they don't give up, we're going to double the amount of tear gas this time. So everybody make sure you have your mask. Some of our people didn't have masks last time. What time do you want to attack, ADA Jefferson?"

"Let's hit them at five thirty."

At five forty-five, the drug task force, including FBI, state, county, city, and the law enforcement team, approached in a convoy of law enforcement vehicles, including heavy-armored SWAT, trucks, and cars, and blocked both entryways to Large International Trucking, Inc. The drug dealers did not expect to see so many law enforcement personnel so soon after the hay farm bust. And they were caught off guard, right in the middle of loading drugs onto their trucks.

Commander Bell used a loudspeaker to demand the drug dealers' surrender. "This is the drug task force, and we have a warrant to search every building, vehicle, and person at this location. Put your hands on your heads, and in a single line, start walking toward the entryway. Do not attempt to remove any items from this facility. When an officer requests identification from you, that is the only time that you may take your hands off your head. Start to walk this way now."

Drivers in three of the eighteen-wheelers started the engines and began driving as fast as they could toward the law enforcement vehicles blocking the entryways. And at the same time, the other drug dealers began shooting with AR-15s, AK-47s, M16, shotguns, and other types of weapons.

Pop, pop, pop, pop, pop, pop, pop, pop, pop, pop, pop!

Law enforcement personnel returned fire, and they fired tear gas from the ground. Helicopters dropped tear gas from the sky.

Boom! Boom! Boom! Boom! Boom! Boom! Pop, pop, pop, pop, pop, pop! Boom! Boom! Boom! Pop, pop, pop, pop, pop, pop!

One of the drivers in an eighteen-wheeler was shot and killed, and as a result, the truck went out of control and flipped several times, throwing heroin and pills through the air. Suddenly another eighteen-wheeler truck crashed into law enforcement vehicles attempting to open the blocked entryway, but it was not successful. The driver was shot and killed as the gunfight continued.

Boom! Boom! Boom! Pop, pop, pop, pop, pop, pop! Boom! Boom! Boom! Pop, pop, pop, pop, pop, pop!

Eighteen-wheelers were trying to leave, but the gunfire was too much. A helicopter was hit by gunfire several times and crashed into the office complex.

Kaboom!

The complex caught fire, and men started running out of the building. But the gunfight continued.

Boom! Boom! Boom! Pop, pop, pop, pop, pop, pop! Boom! Boom! Boom! Pop, pop, pop, pop, pop, pop! Boom! Boom! Boom! Boom! Boom! Boom!

An eighteen-wheeler rammed the police line.

The police officer yelled, "Look out! He's going to ram us!"

Bam! Boom! Boom! Boom! Pop, pop, pop, pop, pop, pop! Boom! Boom! Boom! Pop, pop, pop, pop, pop, pop! Boom! Boom! Boom! Boom! Boom! Boom!

The gun battle went on for several hours, but the drug dealers couldn't take it anymore. They finally surrendered.

"We've had enough. We give up! Stop shooting. We quit! We quit!"

Commander Bell spoke into the loudspeaker. "Cease fire! Throw down your weapons and put your hands above your head. Throw down your weapons. Line up in a single line and walk toward the entryway. When they get here, handcuff them, and put them on the bus. Keep moving. Let's go. Take care of all our injured officers first."

ADA Jefferson congratulated his colleagues. "You did a great job, Commander Bell. Detective Littleton, you did a good job. Call Ms. Jackson and tell her we've got at least a hundred and fifty more coming."

Detective Littleton shared some bad news. "I'll do it. Did you hear about Detective Mitchell? He was shot and killed."

ADA Jefferson hated to hear it. "Got-damn! What about Detective Phillips? Is he ok?"

Detective Littleton continued, "He was hit, but it's not life threatening. Are you ok?"

"I could use a good drink."

Detective Littleton smiled. "Yeah, you're ok."

They both laughed.

ADA Jefferson continued to work. "We've got to get the fires out before we lose some evidence. Let's get these vehicles moved so we can get the fire engines in here." He decided to call DA Adam Winston.

"This is ADA Jefferson, and I figured you'd be still in the office at nine thirty. We got them, and we're putting them in cuffs and loading them on the bus to take them to jail."

DA Winston was pleased with the report. "Tell everyone I said good job."

The following day, ADA Jefferson asked his secretary to schedule a law enforcement team meeting for one o'clock in interrogation room one. "And schedule inmate Barney Henderson to be brought to that same room at one thirty."

ADA Jefferson opened the meeting. "We lost a good man yesterday. Narcotics Lead Detective Bobby Mitchell always gave his best effort, and that's all any of us can to do. But the war against crime goes on, and we've got to keep fighting. I'm happy to welcome to the team Nancy Beckman, the new narcotics lead detective. Welcome to the team."

"Thank you. I'm looking forward to working with each of you."

ADA Jefferson kept his eyes on the target. "Now back to the work. As all of you know, we've just accomplished the three largest drug busts in the history of not just this state but the entire nation. The most important question has not been answered. How are they getting these drugs into our country? We know it's coming from Russia, but how? Our most important informant is being brought here as we speak, and I'm expecting him to give us that answer."

Four officers arrived with Barney Henderson and his attorney. They took their seats, and the officers waited in the corridor.

ADA Jefferson applied pressure. "Barney, we want to know exactly how the Russians are moving drugs from their country to our cities."

Barney Henderson was resisting, "I've given you good information, and you've made a big bust. I think I've done my job."

ADA Jefferson was in no mood for delays. "Ask your attorney what happens when you stop answering my questions. Ask him what happens."

Lenny F. Williams explained what was at stake. "Barney, the agreement states that if you fail to answer any of the questions or if you fail to answer truthfully, the agreement is cancelled. And you go back in to the general prison population, and the death penalty is back on the table."

Barney Henderson knew there was a contract on him and he wouldn't survive one hour in the general population in or out of prison.

So he began to tell what he knew. "They use cruise ships. Any cruise ship coming in from Russia could be loaded with opiates. And once they get it here, they use eighteen-wheelers to take it all over the country."

ADA Jefferson asked, "Does anyone else have questions for this prisoner?"

Detective Beckman was inquisitive. "How do they transfer the dope from the ships to the trucks?"

"The drug dealers are dressed as part of the maintenance crew, and after all of the passengers are off the boat, late at night it appears that they're doing maintenance, but they're actually moving dope."

ADA Jefferson liked that information. "That's good to know. Are there any more questions?"

Detective Littleton was one of the most experienced detectives. "What's the name of the cruise lines that are carrying the dope?"

"Russia's Finest, From Russia with Love, and the Best of Russia."

Detective Phillips joined in. "Are they carrying dope every time they come in?"

Barney Henderson kept talking. "The only way you'll know is when they park those trucks a day or two in advance of the ship's arrival."

Detective Phillips continued, "Where are they docking?"

"The ships are docking at the international port of Los Angeles and the international port of San Francisco."

ADA Jefferson got more out of his witness. "I want to know the names of the trucking lines."

"Big Freeze Trucking Line and Polar Bear Express Trucking Line."

ADA Jefferson believed they had enough. "Are there any more questions? If not, you can go back now, Barney."

ADA Jefferson walked to the door, opened it, and told the officers to take Barney Henderson back to his cell. After Henderson and his attorney were out, ADA Jefferson walked back to his chair, sat down, and continued the meeting.

"Ok, let's look at everything we've learned before we call the next drug task force meeting. This next bust is going to be so big that we're going to run out of space to store the dope and the prisoners."

They all laughed!

Detective Phillips shared his thoughts. "This is going to be a hell of a gunfight. And I'll tell you something else. We've lost two assistant district attorneys in less than a year. So we're going to have to be on our toes because we're talking about billions of dollars and tons of drugs."

ADA Jefferson joked with Detective Phillips, "Well, Phillips, I appreciate you constantly reminding us that this is the real drug war, not that war on drugs that politicians like to play. We've buried a lot of bodies, and we're going to have to bury some more. What's the alternative? Turn the country over to Russia? I can't speak Russian."

They all laughed!

ADA Jefferson kept his eyes on the target. "I'll schedule a drug task force meeting for tomorrow at ten o'clock in the district attorney's conference room. And we'll organize for the upcoming drug bust. You know we couldn't make it in this business without reliable informants. I'll tell you I wanted Barney Henderson dead after the murder of ADA Sanchez, but look at what we would have missed if we'd killed this guy."

ADA Jefferson called and asked his secretary to schedule a drug task force meeting for the following day at 10:00 a.m. in the district attorney's conference room.

The following morning, ADA Jefferson opened the drug task force meeting and informed the group that they were about to face their greatest challenge. "I think most of you are aware that Lead Narcotics Detective Bobby Mitchell was one of the law enforcement officials killed during our last operation. And all of us know that in the law enforcement business, in a situation like this, it's always the next person in line that makes it possible for crime fighting to continue.

"With that being said, I want to introduce everyone to the new lead narcotics detective, Nancy Beckman. And in her position, she becomes a permanent member of the law enforcement team and the drug task force. Welcome aboard, Detective Beckman. This is the first time we've met since the Large International Trucking, Inc., takedown.

"That bust—combined with the Breaks Hay Farm and the college busts—represents some of the most effective crime fighting that's gone on in this nation. Homicide Lead Detective Virgil Phillips constantly reminds us that we're hurting the Russian mob and their American supporters really bad, and as a result, the possibility of retaliation is going to increase. So we really need to be on our toes going forward. This is really critical at this moment because our next bust will make the last two look like child's play. We've learned through our informant how the Russians are bringing drugs into the country. They're using cruise ships as a cover to haul thousands of tons of heroin and pills."

Commander Bell wanted to hear more. "You're not suggesting that these guys are going to try to use the passengers as human shields, are you?"

ADA Jefferson responded, "No, not if we play it right. According to our informant, they'll dock the ships and unload the passengers. And during normal maintenance hours, approximately eleven at night, that's when they unload the drugs."

Commander Bell was relieved. "That's great because, as you know, we're always attempting to minimize civilian casualties."

ADA Jefferson continued, "We were told that there are two main ports, the international port of Los Angeles and the international port of San Francisco, receiving drugs. So obviously we've got to coordinate with those state and local officials."

Agent Holly offered input. "The FBI can be a real asset on that. It's just going to be a matter of us getting our date, time, and location issues worked out. That also includes specific target identification and getting that information into the hands of our LA and San Francisco offices. That'll get everybody on the same clock and watching the same targets."

ADA Jefferson continued, "In reference to specific targets, there are three cruise ship lines that dock in both cities that are the drug carriers: Russia's Finest, The Best of Russia, and From Russia with Love. We've got to get their schedules."

Detective Phillips offered critical guidance. "When we request these schedules, there's some risk of exposing ourselves because if these Russians are hauling tons of drugs into these ports on a regular basis, some port employees have to be aware of it. They could tip off the Russians that law enforcement is making a move."

Detective Beckman had a question. "Wouldn't the Coast Guard have to have the shipping schedules? And shouldn't they be more likely to keep our secrets?"

Agent Holly agreed. "I think the Coast Guard is a splendid recommendation. It keeps civilians from being involved. Also since we're going to be fighting on the water, they can be a great asset. I can make contact with them on behalf of the task force."

ADA Jefferson continued, "There are some trucking lines that are working in conjunction with the cruise ship lines. The Polar Bear Express Trucking Line covers the LA port. And the Big Freeze Trucking Line covers the San Francisco port."

Agent Holly recited the information. "So we've got cruise ship lines, trucking lines, and port operations that are implicated so far."

Detective Beckman added critical input. "And it includes wherever the truck's headquarters are, their destinations with the drugs, and whoever receives and disseminates the drugs from there."

Agent Holly commented, "Those are very good points, Detective. So when we commandeer the ships and trucks, the word is going to spread like wildfire, which means we're looking at the need to hit five targets at once."

Commander Bell concurred. "I get your point, but we may have to limit our scope initially. Once we secure the major targets which are—and correct me if I'm wrong—the shipping lines, trucking line headquarters, and port authority in both cities."

Detective Beckman joined in. "Once we get those guys, we can force the trucking company to tell us where they're taking the dope, or else they spend the rest of their lives in prison."

ADA Robert Jefferson was thinking that this was the best drug task force meeting they'd ever had. He loved the interaction from each member.

Detective Beckman continued, "The trucking lines are the connection between the mob boss and the street."

ADA Jefferson discussed the approach. "Sounds like we may need to phase this bust. For instance in phase one, we put the ships and trucks out of business."

Commander Bell raised a question. "But aren't the port authorities as important as the ships and trucks? I feel strongly that the Russians couldn't do this without the cooperation of the port authorities. And I propose that we add port authorities to phase one of the plan."

Detective Phillips provided insight. "We're at a point in our investigation that we can make a bust on the ships and trucks right now. And we've got to move because there's a time factor as a result of our previous success. We've got to hit them before the drug bosses get spooked and change their routine. Once we get the ships and trucks, we can get the others."

ADA Jefferson agreed with Detective Phillips. "Time is a factor because if we don't get the ships, we have nothing. Once we get the ships, we've got everything. But I suggest that we wiretap the phones at the shipping headquarters, trucking headquarters, and ports immediately."

Agent Holly volunteered. "I'll take care of all the wiretaps today."

ADA Jefferson followed up. "I'll get an email to you with everything you need for the probable cause. Can we be ready to move in seventy-two hours?"

Commander Bell concurred. "Yes, we can do it."

Agent Holly agreed with the time frame. "Yes, we can do it in seventy-two hours. As soon as this meeting is over, I'm going to get on the phone, making calls and setting everything in motion."

ADA Jefferson continued, "Here's the key to everything. Every ship may not have drugs, but the thing that signals when the drugs are coming are the trucks. They will arrive twenty-four to forty-eight hours at the docks before the drug ships arrive with the drugs. Once we see the trucks in place, we know a drug shipment is about to arrive. They always unload the drugs at approximately eleven o'clock. We'll see eighteen-wheelers pulling into position near the ships at about that time. Today, we need the schedules for the ships, and we need to start monitoring the ports immediately. And based on what the schedules tell us, we'll adjust our strike date.

"At this point, we don't know the exact date the drugs will arrive, but the shipping schedules and trucking movement will help us with that. We do know whatever date we determine the bust will happen.

It will take place at approximately eleven o'clock on that date. If there is nothing else, we'll conclude this meeting. And I'm looking forward to executing this operation. If you need anything from me, you can contact me at any time, day or night."

Detectives Phillips, Littleton, and Beckman were about to go to lunch.

Detective Phillips commented, "ADA Jefferson is doing a damn good job."

Detective Littleton agreed. "Yeah, ever since we lost ADA Sanchez, he's hit the ground running."

Detective Beckman shared an observation. "And did you notice that he keeps his gun with him at all times?"

Detective Phillips responded, "Yeah, he better because he'll need it with the type of criminals we're fighting."

They all laughed and went to lunch.

Approximately eighty-six hours since the last meeting, ADA Jefferson was in his hotel room in Los Angeles when he received a call from Agent Holly.

"This is Agent Holly. As you are aware, the shipping schedules that we acquired indicated that the drug trafficker's cruise ships would be arriving on Friday this week. We've got additional confirmation on that. Our surveillance teams observed Polar Bear Express Trucking Lines' eighteen-wheelers parking in close proximity to the international port of Los Angeles. And Big Freeze Trucking Lines' eighteen-wheelers are parking in close proximity to the international port of San Francisco."

ADA Jefferson was pleased with the news. "That's great to hear."

On Friday night, at approximately 11:00 p.m., the multi-state drug task force, including the FBI, Coast Guard Air and Water, state, county, city, and the law enforcement team, were ready to strike. The cruise ships were docked. All of the passengers and their luggage were off the ships. The eighteen-wheelers had moved into place, and the heroin and opiate pills were being unloaded from the ships and loaded onto the trucks.

The drug task force at the international port of Los Angeles burst into action. Law enforcement vehicles, including SWAT vans, police cars, FBI vans, and Coast Guard boats on the water, sped into place. The men and women officers leapt from the vehicles with protective gear on and weapons drawn. They took cover behind vehicles. The drug traffickers were shocked.

The task force commander, with a loudspeaker in hand, gave a command to the drug dealers. "Don't anybody move. Stop what you are doing, and put your hands up. Walk toward the law enforcement vehicles in a single line."

The drug dealer's security team started shooting, and law enforcement returned fire.

The task force commander called over the intercom for air support. "Don't wait! Drop the tear gas right now and keep it coming!"

Boom! Boom! Boom! Pop, pop, pop, pop, pop, pop! Boom! Boom! Boom! Pop, pop, pop, pop, pop, pop! Boom! Boom! Boom! Boom! Boom! Boom!

Helicopters were flying overhead back and forth, dropping tear gas while bullets were flying from both sides. The port had been transformed into a war zone.

Boom! Pop, pop, pop, pop, pop, pop! Boom! Boom! Boom! Boom! Boom! Boom!

A Coast Guard helicopter was hit by a .50-caliber machine gun that was being fired from one of the ships. The pilot was killed instantly, and the helicopter began to smoke and splash into the ocean.

Kaboom!

The crew was killed.

Boom! Pop, pop, pop, pop, pop, pop! Boom! Boom! Boom! Boom! Boom! Boom! Pop, pop, pop, pop, pop, pop! Boom! Boom! Boom!

The drug dealers who were loading the trucks began to surrender, but the ones on the ships, who were heavily armed, continued to fire.

Boom! Pop, pop, pop, pop, pop, pop! Boom! Boom! Boom! Boom! Boom! Boom!

The Coast Guard used loudspeakers to warn the drug dealers on the ships that if they didn't surrender, they would receive cannon fire. Two of the large ships began to move and maneuver, striking the dock, but still managed to get turned and headed out into the ocean. A Coast

Guard boat acting as a blockade was seconds away from being rammed by an escaping cruise ship.

Bam!

The Coast Guard boat, with two dead crewmembers and others injured, started to sink.

Boom! Pop, pop, pop, pop, pop, pop! Boom! Boom! Boom! Boom! Boom! Boom! Pop, pop, pop, pop, pop, pop!

Three Coast Guard helicopters were in hot pursuit of the escaping cruise ships as they exchanged fire.

Pop, pop, pop, pop! Boom! Boom! Boom! Boom! Boom! Boom!

The drug task force had control of the eighteen-wheelers, but the machine gun fire from the ships was making the situation more dangerous.

Agent Holly used the intercom and called for more support. "Tell those Coast Guard gunners to fire those cannons and knock out those damn machine guns!"

Boom! Boom! Boom! Boom! Boom! Boom! Boom! Boom! Boom! Boom! Boom! Boom! Kaboom! Kaboom!

After the cannon fire, the drug dealers on the ships at the docks surrendered. All that was left was to catch the two cruise ships attempting to escape in the ocean. They were being hit hard by cannon fire from the helicopters, and they were too slow to escape.

Boom! Kaboom!

There was an explosion on one of the fleeing cruise ships.

Kaboom! Kaboom!

After two more explosions, the ship started to blaze. It was over. Both ships were on fire, and the drug dealers on board surrendered.

Agent Holly received a call from the FBI office in San Francisco.

"This is Agent John Johnson, San Francisco office. Just wanted you to know that they put up a fight, but we got them."

Agent Holly was pleased with the news. "Same here! Since you're in the office, would you give the order for our agents to proceed with the arrest of the owners of both trucking lines?"

Agent Johnson concurred. "I'll do it. I hear you guys had a hell of a gunfight in L.A."

"If we didn't have those Coast Guard cannons, we'd still be fighting. I better go. Thanks for the support."

ADA Jefferson made a call to DA Winston.

"ADA Robert Jefferson here, and I just wanted you to know we got them."

DA Winston was overjoyed with the news. "I knew you would. Are Detectives Phillips, Littleton, and Beckman ok?"

"Yes, everyone is fine."

DA Winston could relax now. "Tell them I said good job, and I'm very proud of the way you represent this office."

ADA Jefferson continued, "I'll tell them, and we'll see you next week. Have a good weekend."

ADA Jefferson opened the Wednesday morning law enforcement team meeting. "I thought it would be a good idea for us to just talk about Friday's bust and where we go from here. Let me say that it's good to see everyone healthy. Let's just talk about what we're thinking."

Detective Beckman offered her thoughts. "As a narcotics detective, I thought I'd just about seen everything, but I've never seen that much dope in my life. And the level of resistance was surprising. The fact that they were so well armed was surprising. I've been in gunfights before, but that was a war zone."

Detective Littleton joined in. "That's how we lost Detective Mitchell. It was a very similar shootout except for all the water, boats, and ships. They fought like hell at the hay farm and the trucking company. Detective Phillips took a bullet at the trucking company shootout."

Detective Phillips offered his thoughts. "We've done amazing work, and we've made some real enemies. But I don't think you can let up on these guys. Once you start this kind of enforcement, you have to keep your foot on their necks. And here's how we hurt them in ways that we may have not fully considered.

"Sure we're sending a lot of them to prison, we've killed a lot of them, and we've confiscated tons of drugs. And that hurt them. But what they're really worried about is that so many people that we have incarcerated can testify about what they know, which means they can't use the same methods ever again. They've got a lot of thinking to do to try to get back what they had. We can be proud of what we accomplished because they're hurting big time this morning. What's strange is this history-making drug bust started with one junkie in a fight with his supplier.

"Another thing is the law enforcement partnership that enabled all of this success. We worked together at every level of government: federal, state, county, and city. I've never experienced that level of cooperation before. So what are you thinking, ADA Jefferson?"

"I'm like you guys. The adrenalin is rushing through my body. But I do agree with Detective Phillips. Once you hit like this, it never goes back to business as usual. This is the new normal when it comes to crime fighting. We've developed a zero tolerance for drug dealers. That zero tolerance especially applies to Russian drug dealers flooding our country with this poison. We've sent the right message. And I know I've got a lot of court work too and we've got a lot of reports to write, but the high standard that we've established makes me hungry for the next bust. I also think it's important for us to have these cool-down sessions after so much action because there's the real possibility for post-traumatic stress.

"We're human. Philips has been shot, Beckman lost a division chief who was our close colleague, and we've lost two great ADAs. And Littleton, you've been in four consecutive busts and three shootouts. It's not normal for robbery detectives to be around so much killing, is it?"

"What you're saying is completely true. I'm still unwinding from it all. When you're in the action shooting and being shot at, you're just in the moment. Kill or be killed. I've thought about ADA Sanchez being shot down at her front door and ADA Davis being murdered in her home. My thoughts have been that we can't let the bad guys get away with it. We've got to do it for the fallen officers. We've got to do it for the civilians that we're sworn to protect. And we've got to do it because we can't let the bastards have the last word. The streets have to be safe, and it's our job to make sure that they are. So I'm in all the way.

"And what Phillips said is true: this thing started with one junkie, and at the time, I was investigating a church robbery. And from that one junkie, it progressed to four major drug busts. It's the most interesting thing I've ever experienced in my entire life."

Detective Beckman added her thoughts. "I feel like I need to say something about Detective Bobby Mitchell. I was shocked when I first got word that he was gone. He was my mentor, and he'd shared everything he knows about the job with me. He made my work simpler because sometimes things can get so complex, but just the sharing of information makes it simpler. I feel that same way about you guys.

"Ever since I stepped into Detective Mitchell's shoes, I've had to adjust to the fact that the person is gone and at the same time taking on the additional responsibilities. And things seem to be happening so fast that it could have been hard to balance. But the way you brought me into the team made me feel that I had nothing to prove and didn't have to earn anything. I was just a team member, and there was no probation period. It was just we're all in this together. That was important to me because struggling with the loss of a colleague and coping to learn new personalities could have caused some uncertainty in my mind. But the way you guys welcomed me in as if you knew me and worked with me forever, I appreciate it. Especially you, ADA Jefferson, the way you go about the business with nothing but the business in mind is good to see. There's no working through ego or personality. It's just the work. That's refreshing, and I appreciate it from you and everyone in this room."

ADA Jefferson responded, "I think it's really important that in our line of work we not have any unnecessary distractions. Quite honestly, in this business, it can literally get you killed. I work better when I'm relaxed, and I assume that's true about everyone. There's a good chance things are going to get tougher, as our homicide expert always reminds us, so we have to know that we are together as a team. The criminals have to know that if you mess with one of us, you're messing with us all. And we're going to get you no matter how long it takes, and it's not going to take that long. And I tell you why I say that, after what we've gone through, I feel like I'm a better law enforcement officer.

"And I'll be honest with you. I look forward to every meeting because it's an opportunity to grow in this business. To hear all of you experts interact, exchanging ideas and sharing expertise, I'm like a sponge—everything from jail administration, homicide, robbery, and narcotics. We've got the FBI and state in the room. It makes me a wiser law enforcement official. What's interesting is that you can learn things through a conversation in one day that could otherwise take you twenty years to learn, if you learn it at all.

"I do know this: we've got a lot done in a short period of time. And as a result, we're a stronger and better unit. We know we haven't solved all of the world's problems, but the work we've accomplished has repercussions all around. It gives people hope that they can succeed at a much higher level than they might have imagined. The Russian mob understands that they're facing a law enforcement team like they've never faced before. And they know as long as they're committing crimes in this country, we'll be coming after them."

Meanwhile in New York, the FBI was at the home of George McMaster, owner, president, and CEO of Big Freeze Trucking Line, with a no-knock arrest warrant.

Bam!

The door flew open, and there were several pieces of luggage sitting in the living room as if someone were about to leave for vacation.

Mrs. Judy McMaster was sitting on the sofa when the lawmen entered, and she was shocked. "Don't shoot! Don't shoot! I'll tell you whatever you want to know!"

Agent Oliver Norton took charge. "Stand up and put your hands behind your back. Put handcuffs on her. Where's your husband?"

"He's in the bathroom in the back."

At that moment, two more FBI agents entered the room with George McMaster wearing handcuffs.

The FBI agent explained, "We caught him slipping out the backdoor."

Agent Norton advanced the process. "Read them their rights. Search the entire house and garage. Mr. and Mrs. McMaster, where's your kids?"

The McMasters didn't respond.

Agent Norton continued, "You don't have to tell us. We'll find them, and when we do, they'll be arrested."

Agent Joe Jackson read the McMasters their rights. "You have the right to remain silent. Anything you say will be used against you. You have the right to an attorney, and if you cannot afford one, an attorney will be appointed to you. Do you understand the rights that I've just read to you?"

Both prisoners said yes.

Agent Norton made arrangements for transport. "Make sure you put them in separate cars."

While FBI agents were serving the warrant at the McMaster home, another team of FBI agents was serving a warrant at Big Freeze Trucking Line headquarters and related properties.

Agent Norton made a phone call to Agent Holly. "This is Agent Oliver Norton in New York. We've arrested George and Judy McMaster."

Agent Holly was pleased with the news. "That's great news. What's the jurisdictional priority there in New York? Do you guys file charges there, or do we get them first?"

Agent Norton responded, "The district attorney will determine that, as you know we agents investigate and arrest but lawyers prosecute. But I wanted you to know we got them. There's also a team of FBI agents at the house and business of Bud Dixon, owner and CEO of Polar Bear Express Trucking Line."

Agent Holly appreciated the information. "Thanks for the information. I'll pass it on."

Agent Norton continued, "I want to compliment you guys for the work in New Mexico, Los Angeles, and San Francisco."

"Thanks. We'll keep fighting until the fight is over."

Agent Holly, who was at his New Mexico office, called ADA Jefferson's cell phone. ADA Jefferson was on the way to interrogation room one to meet with the law enforcement team and their informant, Barney Henderson. Henderson's attorney, Lenny F. Williams, would be present also.

"This is Agent Holly. I want you to know the FBI in the New York office have arrested George McMaster and his wife, Judy. George is owner, president, and CEO of Big Freeze Trucking Line. They're also in the process of arresting Bud Dixon and his wife. They own the Polar Bear Express Trucking Line."

A big smile came on the face of ADA Robert Jefferson. "That's great news. I'll pass it on to the team. I'm heading to a meeting at this very moment. Thanks."

The law enforcement team was part of the most successful drug-fighting force in the history of the nation, but they wouldn't be satisfied until they arrested the boss of the Russian mob and all of his American partners. The team was meeting with their informant, Barney Henderson, and his attorney.

ADA Robert Jefferson shared the news with the team. "I just got off the phone with Agent Holly. He confirmed that those two trucking line targets have been apprehended."

The team gave each other high-fives.

ADA Jefferson continued, "Tell the officers to bring in the prisoner."

Two officers escorted Barney Henderson and his attorney into the interrogation room.

ADA Jefferson questioned the prisoner, "What can you tell us about this Russian mob boss, and where can we find him?"

Kaboom! Kaboom!

Detective Phillips, like the rest of the team, was shocked by an explosion. "What the hell was that?"

Detective Beckman offered her opinion. "Sounded like an explosion!"

Detective Phillips' cell phone rang. "Detective Phillips speaking."

"This is dispatch. A bomb just exploded in the district attorney's office."

Detective Phillips was ready to go to work. "I'm on the way." He shared the news with the team. "That was dispatch. A bomb just exploded at the district attorney's office."

ADA Jefferson reacted. "That got-damn mob! Did anybody get killed?"

"They didn't say."

The team got up and headed out the door.

ADA Robert Jefferson yelled instructions, "Officers, take this prisoner back to his cell."

The fire trucks had arrived, and the firefighters were working to extinguish the blaze. The law enforcement team was standing outside on the adjacent sidewalk at a safe distance, staring in disbelief at what was left of the district attorney's office. ADA Jefferson realized that DA Winston had been killed in this bombing, and now he was the next-ranking official in that office. As a result, he was even more determined to take down the Russian mob.

"Detective Phillips, you're going to have to take the lead on this one."

"No problem. I've got it. The hay farm owner was caught trying to run to Russia. That makes me think he knows something, and I'm going to talk to him and his wife today."

Detective Philips made a call to Dianne Jackson. "This is Detective Virgil Phillips, and I need Mr. and Mrs. Howard B. Sharks brought to interrogation rooms one and two as soon as possible. And I need Barney Henderson in interrogation room three. Thank you."

"They will be there in forty-five minutes."

Detective Phillips informed the team, "I've got Howard B. Sharks coming to interrogation room one, and his wife will be in two. Barney Henderson will be in three."

Acting DA Robert Jefferson said, "Yeah, let's do it." He then called Agent Holly.

"This is Acting DA Robert Jefferson. I wanted to make sure you're aware of the bombing at the district attorney's office. I also want to confirm whether DA Adam Winston is deceased as a result of that booming."

Agent Holly hated to hear about the murder of the third person in that office. "I was about to head over there."

Acting DA Jefferson was walking while he spoke. "The team and I will be at the police station interrogating prisoners."

Agent Holly was on the way out the door. "Ok, I'll let you know if I learn anything."

Detective Phillips called Detective Corns. "This is Phillips. Stay on top of the bombing at the district attorney's office. I'm going to be questioning prisoners trying to get a lead."

After getting back to the interrogation rooms, the team talked to Mrs. Hattie Sharks first.

Detective Phillips opened the questioning. "I can get you out of here, and you'll never have to come back."

"I helped you before, and I didn't get anything for it. I gave you Henderson!"

Detective Phillips explained, "A lot of law enforcement personnel have died, but I assure you that if you tell us everything you know about the Russians and it leads to arrest, we'll set you free, and you'll never have to come back."

Mrs. Hattie Sharks pointed the finger to her husband. "My husband is the Russian lover. He talks with them all the time. He should be able to tell you everything you want to know."

Acting DA Jefferson made a promise. "I'm going to recommend bail to the judge because you have been so helpful. We got so busy that I haven't had a chance to get to it, but I will. Have the officers take Mrs. Sharks back to her cell."

The team left interrogation room one and entered room three. Barney Henderson and his attorney, Lenny F. Williams, were there under guard. As the team entered, the officers stepped out into the corridor.

Detective Phillips got very direct. "Where is the Russian mob headquarters located, and what's the name of the mob boss?"

Barney Henderson repeated himself. "Like I told you before, this is a Russian operation, and you better believe that they are mad as hell and they are going to hit back. You took down their main moneymaker, and you expect them to just roll over and go away. That's not going to happen."

Acting DA Jefferson intervened. "Stop wasting our got-damn time. Answer the man's questions!"

Barney Henderson got nervous. "I don't have that information, but you have the guy who does. His name is Howard B. Sharks, and he meets face-to-face with the Russians all the time."

Acting DA Jefferson ordered officers to take Barney Henderson back to his cell. The team exited interrogation room three and entered room two. Howard B. Sharks and his attorney were there waiting under guard. The officers left the room.

Detective Phillips got it started. "Tell us everything you know about the Russian mob's operation in this country. Give us that, and your wife can avoid prosecution."

Howard B. Sharks started smart-talking. "What's the problem? Barney didn't tell you everything you needed?"

Acting DA Jefferson put Sharks in his place. "Let me tell you something. Your Russian buddies killed our district attorney today. That means I'm the district attorney now. Your entire family is incarcerated, and they can't get access to any of that drug money you got. They're sitting in jail just like you. I'm the only one that can make favorable recommendations on their behalf. So are you sure that you want to sit here and talk smart to me?"

Howard B. Sharks felt the fear. "Ok, I'll help, but I want my family out of jail. The big boss was in Chicago. But I know he knows my wife and me have been arrested. And he knows about the West Coast drug bust. So he's probably on the move."

Acting DA Jefferson pressured Shark. "I want his name and the address of his office and home in Chicago."

"The home is at 27007 Riverdale. The office is at 45066 White Oak Trail. His name is Morris Borkoff."

Acting DA Jefferson took out his cell phone and called Agent Holly. He repeated everything that Howard B. Sharks shared with him. Then he said, "He's probably on the run."

"I'll call the Chicago office right now, and I'll start a nationwide manhunt."

Agent Holly made contact with the Chicago FBI and provided all the information.

Acting DA Robert Jefferson pursued additional information from the Sharks. "Where would he run to? Where are his contacts?"

"His main safe contacts are too hot for him, and they're no longer safe. And that's Chicago and your city. There's an Illinois congressman named Homer Page who's been taking Russian money. He has a home in Chicago, but he also has a farmhouse. He could be helping Borkoff run."

Acting DA Jefferson called the FBI again. "Acting DA Robert Jefferson here. I just got word of an Illinois congressman named Homer Page. He is believed to be on Morris Borkoff's payroll. He has a home in Chicago, and he also owns a farmhouse."

"I'll make the call."

Agent Holly called the Chicago FBI office and informed them of Congressman Homer Page.

Acting DA Jefferson continued the interrogation of Howard B. Sharks. "Can you think of any place else this guy might be getting some assistance?"

"The way you've been coming after Borkoff's operation, his old hideaways aren't safe for him. So he's going to be looking for a new connection."

Detective Beckman had a new angle. "What's his woman's name?"

Howard B. Sharks seemed surprised at the question. "Natasha Pam. She lives in Chicago."

Acting DA Robert Jefferson called the FBI with the latest information. "Acting DA Robert Jefferson. Morris Borkoff has a woman in Chicago named Natasha Pam. We don't have an address."

Agent Holly wrote a note. "I'll make the call."

Agent Holly called the Chicago FBI office and informed them of Natasha Pam. Meanwhile, Morris Borkoff was in the backseat of a limousine. He had two bodyguards and a driver with him, and they were traveling south on Interstate 55, trying to find safety. His goal was to get to Russia, but with the nationwide manhunt, his chances were slim. His driver was doing eighty-seven in a seventy, and a state trooper pulled him over.

The trooper called in the tags and identified Borkoff's name. He then called for help. Morris Borkoff yelled at one of his bodyguards to get out of the car and kill the trooper. Morris Borkoff tried to avoid capture.

"Get out and kill him! Do it now!"

Borkoff's bodyguard quickly opened the door, jumped out of the limousine, aimed his AR-15 automatic weapon at the trooper's car, and began to fire.

Pop, pop, pop, pop, pop, pop, pop, pop, pop, pop, pop, pop!

Before the trooper could pull his handgun and fire back, he was shot five times and died. The bodyguard jumped back into the limousine, and they hurriedly drove away. Morris Borkoff knew he had to get to the West Coast, so he ordered his driver to get off Interstate 55.

"Make a right up here onto Interstate 70."

Morris Borkoff made a phone call to one of his main contacts, Congressman Homer Page. "This is Borkoff. Where is Natasha?"

The question puzzled the congressman. "I don't know. I haven't heard from anyone. Where are you?"

Morris Borkoff didn't give his location. "I'm looking for a friend."

Homer Page knew that response was a code, meaning Borkoff was on the run. "Have you talked to Sprawling? He took care of that thing you wanted done in New Mexico."

Morris Borkoff wanted more. "We need to kill Harold B. Sharks, Hattie Sharks, and Barney Henderson tomorrow."

The congressman called Chief Jack Sprawling, who was at his desk in New Mexico's police station. "This is Homer. He's not satisfied with the work you did. He wants Harold B. Sharks, Hattie Sharks, and Barney Henderson dead tomorrow."

Chief Jack Sprawling knew it was going to be complicated. "Look, my boys will do anything I tell them to do, but we need to move with some caution."

Homer Page reemphasized the order. "He said he wants it done tomorrow."

Chief Sprawling was thinking it over. "I might be able to get one or two of them tomorrow, but it's going to take a while to get them all.

You know they hurt our business big time, so they got to pay the price. Where's he at?"

Congressman Page was anxious to get off the phone. "He said he's looking for a friend."

Chief Sprawling had bad intentions. "Where is that fine-ass woman of his?"

"Jack, don't mess with that guy's woman. That's the last thing that should be on your mind."

Chief Sprawling was thinking dangerously. "Hell, she ought to be mine. He don't know what to do with her."

Meanwhile, Natasha Pam got a call from Morris Borkoff. "Come to Little Russia."

Natasha Pam left her hotel room, got in her car, and got on Interstate 70. She headed to Kansas City.

Back in New Mexico, Chief Sprawling was the leader of the local Nazi Party, and some of his people were police officers. Others were prisoners. He used a throwaway phone and made a late-night phone call to the jail.

"Officer Putman speaking."

"This is Jack. I want you to kill prisoners Howard P. Sharks, Hattie Sharks, and Barney Henderson tonight."

At approximately 2:15 a.m., Officer Putman asked Officer Fred Sour, another Nazi, to act as a lookout as he opened the cell doors and allowed four prisoners to come out and follow him into the priority security area. Putman provided knives to each of the men and quietly unlocked three doors. Two prisoners entered Howard B. Sharks' cell and stabbed him to death. Officer Putman entered Hattie Sharks' cell and strangled her to death. Two prisoners entered Barney Henderson's cell and stabbed him to death. The prisoners were allowed to use the officer's washrooms to clean up and then returned to their cells.

Officers Putman and Sour cleaned up the washrooms and put the knives and bloody clothes in a trash bag. Putnam put the bag in the trunk of his car, and he and Sour drove to a dumpster that was a mile east of the jail. He put the trash bag in the dumpster and drove out of the city limits to a Nazi headquarters.

The following morning, all three of the law enforcement team's key witnesses—Howard P. Sharks, Hattie Sharks, and Barney Henderson—were discovered dead in their cells. The law enforcement team was having an emergency meeting.

Acting DA Jefferson was looking for answers. "What's the normal response when you have this kind of problem in your facility?"

Dianne Jackson was feeling the pressure. She'd never had a triple murder in her jail. "There's normally a jail review board that conducts an immediate investigation when you have loss-of-life issues. I've already notified them of the killings. I've got to go and prepare for the meeting with them. I'll keep you updated. But my first thoughts are that this was someone working for the jail. Officers Putman and Sours were not at their duty station this morning."

The jail administrator left the interrogation room. The rest of the team continued assessing the organized violence that was plaguing their city.

Detective Littleton shared her thoughts. "First they kill ADA Sanchez and then the DA. And now they kill our witnesses. We've got to get the bastards."

Detective Phillips concurred. "I've been talking about this all along. It's what Detective Mitchell said, 'With an operation this size, there's no telling who the Russians have purchased.'"

Acting DA Jefferson called the FBI. "This is Acting DA Robert Jefferson. Someone got in our jail and killed all of our witnesses last night. It looks like an inside job. Two of the guards were gone this morning."

Agent Holly was shocked. "Got-damn! There was a state trooper on Interstate 55 who stopped Borkoff last night for speeding in a limousine. The Russians got the jump on him, shot him five times, and killed him. It looks like Borkoff's woman, Natasha Pam, has disappeared. The good news is the Chicago FBI has some men headed out to the congressman's home and farmhouse as we speak. If we're lucky, they'll catch that bastard and get some answers."

"We need that congressman bad. Do you have anything on the bombing?"

"No, but I'll keep you posted."

Acting DA Jefferson continued the meeting. "That was Agent Harold Holly. He said there was a state trooper on Interstate 55 who stopped Borkoff for speeding in a limousine. Borkoff's men got the jump on him, shot him five times, and killed him. Borkoff's woman may have left town. Agent Holly thinks they'll get the congressman. He's our next best witness."

Detective Phillips was analyzing the witness murders. "Morris Borkoff has got somebody on the police force working for him. Those murders in our jail were an inside job. Detective Bobby Mitchell was right. Do you remember when he said, 'With an operation this size, there's no telling who the Russians have bought off'?"

Detective Littleton remembered. "Yeah, I remember what Bobby said."

Detective Beckman expanded the discussion. "If you wanted a cop on your payroll, which cop would you want?"

Detective Phillips took it deeper. "I would want the top cop. What do you think, Littleton?"

"You talked about how the chief's been missing in action and not attending a single drug task force meeting. No job well done or nothing."

Acting DA Jefferson agreed. "We're going to open an official investigation into Chief Jack Sprawling. At some point, we may get the FBI involved, but for now, the four of us are the only ones who need to know about it. I'm going to put a wiretap on his home and office phones."

Detective Phillips was not sure about the wiretaps. "What's your probable cause?"

"You sound like a district attorney."

They all laughed, and Acting DA Jefferson continued, "The probable cause is suspicious conduct and professional negligence based on a lack of participation in all drug task force operations."

Meanwhile in rural Illinois, the FBI was at the home of Congressman Homer Page.

Knock, knock, knock!

The congressman opened the door. His eyes opened wide when he saw the FBI at his door. "Yes, what can I do for you?"

The FBI agent showed the congressman his badge. "I'm Agent Dick Jersey, and I have orders to bring you in to the FBI headquarters for an interview."

The congressman attempted to gather himself. "What is this pertaining to?"

"I'm not authorized to answer any questions. My job is to transport you to the FBI office today. Let's go."

"Can I follow you in my car?"

"No, my orders are to transport you to the FBI office."

Congressman Page was very nervous. "Can I get my phone and wallet?"

"You can get your wallet and phone, but you can't make a call until you get to the FBI office. Two agents will accompany you to get your phone and wallet."

Once the congressman got his phone and wallet, he got in an FBI vehicle with four FBI agents, and they drove to FBI Chicago headquarters and entered the interrogation room.

"I'm Agent Ben Huntsville." He showed his badge and then continued the discussion. "I understand you wanted to call your lawyer. You can do so at this time, but you can't use your phone. The FBI has a warrant for your phone and your home and properties."

The FBI took possession of the congressman's phone, and one of the agents carried it to their lab.

"You can use our phone."

The congressman made his call to his lawyer. "This is Homer. I'm at the FBI headquarters, and I need you here right away."

Attorney Jack D. Franklyn was caught off guard. "What's going on, Homer? Is there a problem?"

The congressman was very nervous. "The FBI wants to ask me some questions. They haven't told me what it's about."

Jack Franklyn was puzzled. "Ok, I'll be there in fifteen minutes."

The FBI waited on the congressman's attorney before asking any questions. While the agents were waiting, back at the congressman's home and property, a team of agents were conducting a thorough search.

Jack Franklyn entered the interrogation room. "Did I miss anything?"

Agent Huntsville responded, "No, you didn't miss anything. We've waited for your arrival before asking any questions. And now that you're here, we'll begin. Congressman Page, explain your relationship with Morris Borkoff."

After hearing the question, Congressman Page was frozen with fear. "I'd like to speak with my attorney in private."

The FBI agents stepped out into the corridor, leaving the congressman and his attorney alone in the room.

Jack Franklyn wanted to know what was going on. "What's this all about, Homer?"

The congressman started to cry. "I've been taking money from this Russian for years. I had no idea anybody knew."

His attorney was concerned about his client. "You can't lie to the FBI. That's a felony, and it'll get you five years in prison. If you don't answer, they'll arrest you, but you can get bail. It may be a couple of days."

The congressman continued, "Do you know how it looks for a congressman to go to jail?"

His attorney explained, "You better believe if they ask the question, they already have the answer. They know you've been taking money. But you're not really who they want. They want the Russian. Help them get the Russian, and they might just let you go free."

Congressman Page was filled with fear. "If I start talking, my life is over. It puts my family in danger. I think I'd rather go to prison than to put my family in danger."

His attorney set Homer straight. "You put yourself and your family in danger when you started taking money from these criminals. You should have known better."

The congressman continued to cry. "If I go to jail, I'm going to get killed today. Did you read about the triple murder in New Mexico? The Russian ordered those killings."

Jack Franklyn was confused about his client's involvement. "What else do you know about that killing?"

"The Russian called me and ordered the murders, and I passed it on to the killer."

Jack Franklyn was shocked. "Got-damn, Homer! You took part in a triple homicide. You might as well have shot them yourself. This is capital murder for the killing of three government witnesses. Your life is over. The best thing you can do is to ask the government to try to protect your family, and the sooner the better."

Congressman Page dried his tears. "Ok, I'm just going to tell them everything. Tell them to come back in."

His attorney opened the door and told the agents that they were ready to talk.

Agent Huntsville repeated the question. "Explain your relationship with Morris Borkoff."

The congressman put both hands over his face and started to cry out loud. And he began to speak. He tried to make special arrangements for his family. "I've got to protect my wife and kids from this Russian. He's a cold-blooded killer, and he's going to try to kill us all. So I need your help to protect my family. The minute he hears that I've been arrested, he'll send some people to kill my family and me."

Agent Huntsville stayed focused. "You didn't answer my question. Explain your relationship with Morris Borkoff."

The congressman, with tears running down his face, admitted the truth. "I've been accepting money from him for years."

Agent Huntsville pressed on. "He gives you money. What do you do for him?"

The congressman was evasive. "I've helped him buy land and start businesses."

Agent Huntsville asked a penetrating question. "The three witnesses who were murdered in New Mexico. Is Morris Borkoff responsible for those deaths?"

Congressman Page couldn't avoid the truth. "Yes, he is."

"How do you know he is responsible?"

The congressman put both hands over his face and started to cry out loud. "He called me and told me that he wanted them dead." He cried some more.

"After Morris Borkoff called you, what did you do?"

Before the congressman could answer, his attorney intervened. "My client needs leniency for all the help you're about to get from him."

Agent Huntsville laid out the facts. "This is a quadruple murder investigation, so if your client helps us solve the murders, he will get maximum consideration. No death penalty, but he will do prison time."

Jack Franklyn gave Homer the go-ahead. "You can continue, Homer."

The congressman stopped crying long enough to speak. "I called the Russian's man in New Mexico."

Agent Huntsville explained that the congressman needed to be more forthcoming. "If you want us to try to save your family, you need to tell us the complete story about every crime you know about, which includes every name and detailed involvement. Who is Morris Borkoff's man in New Mexico?"

Congressman Page cried while speaking. "Chief Jack Sprawling. The chief has a Nazi gang, and they will do anything the chief tells them to do. The chief funds the gang with Russian money that he gets from Morris Borkoff. Morris Borkoff and the chief are responsible for the bombing that killed District Attorney Adam Winston. It was retaliation for the West Coast drug bust."

The Chicago FBI immediately made a phone call to New Mexico to speak with Agent Holly. "This is Agent Ben Huntsville in the Chicago office. You need to immediately arrest Chief Jack Sprawling for the murder of the district attorney there in your city." He then repeated what the congressman had told him.

"I'll get it done right now."

Agent Holly immediately called Acting DA Robert Jefferson, who was in a law enforcement team meeting. He passed along the news of the upcoming arrest. "We picked up Congressman Homer Page, and he just gave us this information. He and the chief work for Morris Borkoff. Morris Borkoff, Congressman Page, Chief Sprawling, and a local Nazi gang are responsible for those deaths of the three witnesses that were murdered in New Mexico. Do you know if the chief is at work today?"

"Hold for a moment. Has anybody seen Chief Sprawling today?"

Detective Littleton responded, "Yeah, I saw him in his office this morning."

Acting DA Jefferson passed on the information to Agent Holly. "Yeah, he's here."

Agent Holly said, "Arrest that murderer and hold him in the interrogation room until I get there."

Acting DA Jefferson informed the team of the current events. Then he said, "Let's go get that murdering bastard."

As they headed to the chief's office, Detective Phillips reacted to the news. "Got-damn, it's just like we thought! Let's go."

While on the way to Chief Sprawling's office, the team requested two officers join them. They arrived at the chief's office, and he was at his desk. The office door was open, and Acting DA Jefferson walked in first. His colleagues were right behind him. Chief Sprawling was taken completely by surprise.

Acting DA Jefferson took charge. "Stand up, Chief. Detective, I want you to put handcuffs on this man. Take his badge and gun and read him his rights."

Detective Phillips followed orders. "Jack Sprawling, you are under arrest for the capital murder of DA Winston and three federal witnesses. You're also being charged with drug trafficking and conspiracy against the United States government. You have the right to remain silent. Anything you say will be used against you in a court of law. You have the right to an attorney. If you can't afford an attorney, one will be assigned to you. Do you understand the rights I've just read to you?"

Chief Jack Sprawling responded, "I understand everything you said."

"Officers, take him to interrogation room one."

The team marched Chief Sprawling, hands behind his back in handcuffs, through the police station, and all of the personnel were shocked to see it, even those who happened to be a part of his Nazi gang. As the team walked to the interrogation room, Detectives Phillips and Littleton reflected on the death toll caused by Chief Sprawling.

Detective Phillips speculated, "This guy probably ordered the hit on ADA Sanchez."

Detective Littleton said, "Add our witness Vicky Swanson to the list."

Detective Beckman joined in. "Hell, Detective Mitchell wouldn't be dead either if it were not for this bastard."

Acting DA Jefferson said, "Put Chief Sprawling in an individual holding cell until the FBI gets here. I want four officers guarding him at all times. Detective Phillips, you're the acting police chief."

Now that they had Chief Sprawling locked up, the team entered interrogation room one. About the time they were seated, Dianne Jackson entered the room and took a seat.

Acting DA Jefferson inquired about the jail investigation. "It's good to see you. How's the investigation progressing?"

"We've identified the ring leaders. It was officers Mike Putman and Fred Sour who left their duty stations. Based on our sources, they let at least four prisoners out of their cells to assist with the killing. We're closing in on the four. We don't know where the two officers are."

Acting DA Jefferson shared the latest news. "We may be able to help you with that soon. The ring leader is Chief Jack Sprawling. He's head of a local Nazi gang, and he commanded your jail staff to do the killing."

Dianne Jackson said, "I was informed that he's in our holding cell."

Acting DA Jefferson replied, "Yeah, his gang is responsible for the bombing death of DA Winston. We also think he could have ordered the death of ADA Sanchez. And he's a major drug trafficker."

Dianne Jackson added, "It looks like we've got our hands full, don't we?"

Detective Phillips said, "I've got to call Detective Corns and tell him he's the acting lead of homicide division." He made the call.

"This is Phillips. I know you've heard about Sprawling, and as a result, I'm acting chief, and you're acting lead."

Detective Corns said, "I understand."

Agent Holly arrived. Acting DA Jefferson assessed the situation. "So we have Jack Sprawling and Homer Page as witnesses, and our goal is to arrest or kill Morris Borkoff. There's also this team of Nazis who carries out the dirty work for Sprawling. So as I see it, our targets are first Borkoff and second the Nazis."

Acting DA Jefferson asked the officers to bring Chief Sprawling to the interrogation room. They brought him in and set him down. His attorney, Lenny F. William, also entered the room. The team was surprised to see that Sprawling had the same attorney as Barney Henderson.

Acting DA Jefferson opened the questioning. "Where are Mike Putman and Fred Sour?"

Lenny F. Williams spoke up for his client. "My client wants some consideration for his assistance."

Acting DA Jefferson said, "Your wife and kids have benefited from drug money, and they're going to be brought in for questioning. And that's my next move if you don't open your murdering mouth and start talking."

Chief Sprawling tried to defend his family, "They don't know anything about my criminal life."

Acting DA Jefferson had no patience for the chief. "You want us to believe the words of a murderer? If you don't tell us where your murdering Nazis are right now, I'm going to initiate an all-points bulletin for your wife and kids so they can tell us what they know." That got Chief Sprawling's attention.

"There's a camp about ten miles south of the city on Interstate 107. You make a right on Hamilton Road. Drive another forty-five minutes and make a left. You drive about two hundred yards, and you're at a metal fence. That's the Nazi compound, and it's about seventy-five men out there."

Acting DA Jefferson pressured Chief Sprawling. "Who is responsible for the district attorney's office bombing?"

"Nazis Billy Further and Johnny Gates did the bombing. I ordered it."

Acting DA Jefferson said, "Agent Holly, as you know, we're trying to identify some killers in our jail system. Can you guys keep this witness safe?"

"Yes, we'll take responsibility for this guy."

Dianne Jackson asked Chief Sprawling to name the four killers. "Who were the prisoners who murdered the witnesses in our jail?"

"Nazis Shawn Beverly, George Evans, Murray Duckworth, and Harry Fields did the killing."

Agent Holly asked Chief Sprawling, "Where's Morris Borkoff?"

"I don't know, but Barney Henderson or Homer Page should know."

Acting DA Jefferson reminded Sprawling of the facts. "Jack Sprawling, you must have forgotten that you murdered Barney Henderson. Are there any more questions for this prisoner? If not, Agent Holly, how do you want to proceed with this murderer?"

"I'm going to call more agents to come over, and we'll take control of him and isolate him until you need him."

Acting DA Jefferson said to the team, "Let's move Jack Sprawling to interrogation room two and keep him under guard until the agents arrive. Agent Holly will remain with him also." Acting DA Jefferson got up from his chair, walked over to the door, opened it, and ordered the officers to move Sprawling to interrogation room two.

The jail administrator made a call and ordered Shawn Beverly, George Evans, Murray Duckworth, and Harry Fields moved to isolated solitary confinement until their murder trial began.

Acting DA Jefferson continued with the meeting. "I think we need to hit that Nazi compound as soon as possible."

Detective Phillips made a recommendation. "Why don't we spend the rest of the day organizing and hit them early in the morning?"

Detective Beckman said, "The longer we wait, the greater the chance they learn that we have their boss. I think we should pull a team together and hit them tonight."

Detective Littleton added, "That's a good point. They know he's at work about now, so they're probably not going to try to contact him at work."

Detective Phillips replied, "We're going to need one hundred and fifty men and air support. Let's do it."

It took a couple of hours to secure the warrant and organize the two hundred-man strike force, including the drug task force, SWAT, FBI, state, county, city, and law enforcement team. And at approximately 7:30 p.m., they were assembled at the main gate of the Nazi compound.

The commander ordered air support to make their move. Commander Bell used the loudspeaker to get started. "Drop that tear gas right on top of them, and I want you to hit them hard and heavy."

Two helicopters swooped down out of the sky, dropping multiple tear gas bombs on the two small buildings housing the gang, and they were caught completely by surprise. The gang had lookouts, but when they saw the helicopters, they panicked and ran inside.

Boom! Boom!

As the helicopters did their job, the SWAT heavy-armored vehicle crashed through the front gate of the compound, and law enforcement vehicles, including vans and trucks, followed right behind. They kept the bus at the gate. All the law enforcement personnel wore gas masks and protective gear, but the Nazis had nothing protecting them from the tear gas. The helicopters continued to bomb the buildings.

Boom! Boom!

The tear gas had blinded the gang members, and they couldn't see or breathe. Some of the officers on the ground began firing tear gas also, and you could barely see the buildings for the smoke.

Boom! Boom!

Commander Bell used a loudspeaker. "You men in the buildings, come out with your hands in the air. Do not bring anything out with you, and do not attempt to escape. Come out with your hands in the air!"

Boom! Boom!

From the air and the ground, the task force continued to bombard both buildings with tear gas.

Boom! Boom!

One of the buildings started to blaze.

"Ok, ok, we'll come out! We can't see! We can't see!"

Commander Bell yelled into the loudspeaker, "Walk out the door with your hands in the air. Now! Cease fire! I think they've had enough!"

The Nazi gang members were walking out the buildings with tears flowing from their eyes. They could barely see.

Commander Bell hollered into the loudspeaker, "Get those buses up here. Get the handcuffs on them, and put them on the bus. Keep them moving!"

Meanwhile in Chicago, the FBI continued questioning Congressman Homer Page.

Agent Huntsville asked, "So you don't have any idea where Borkoff is or where he might be headed?"

"If I knew, I would tell you. My family would be safer if you had this guy locked up. Did you pick up my family yet?"

"Yes, we did."

"Can I see them? They're probably terrified."

Agent Huntsville denied his request. "No, not yet, and if they're terrified, you did it. We've got more questions for you, and we've got questions for them. What's Borkoff's phone number?"

"773-999-9499."

Agent Huntsville called the FBI Technology Tracking Center and provided Borkoff's phone number. He requested a nationwide twenty-four-hour tracking. And he ordered the congressman moved to solitary confinement.

He also called Agent Holly. "This is Agent Ben Huntsville. I wanted to touch base with you before I call it a day. We've got the phone number for that Russian, Morris Borkoff, and there's a nationwide alert. If he uses it, we've got him. That number is 773-999-9499."

"We've just about got him shut down. I think he's trying to get back to Russia. We arrested the Nazi gang that bombed the federal building, so we got those murders solved. When we arrested Jack Sprawling, he gave up the gang right away trying to save his family."

"Yeah, they always try to save their families after they've committed the crime. But if they were really concerned about their families' safety, they wouldn't take that drug money. Once you take it, the drug dealers own you. I'm going to call it a day."

The following day, the FBI Kansas City office got a hit on Morris Borkoff's phone number. A call was made from a suburban home. Someone was trying to get in contact with the congressman.

When the congressman didn't answer, the Russian got nervous and started making plans to relocate as soon as possible. Morris Borkoff panicked and hurriedly prepared to leave.

"Get ready to go. We've got to leave right now!"

Natasha Pam was tired and needed rest. "We've got to leave again? We just got here."

"The police are on the way here right now. Let's go. We don't have time to pack!"

Morris Borkoff, Natasha Pam, the driver, and two bodyguards rushed into the limousine and drove away. Fifteen minutes later, the local FBI rushed to the address where the call was made. The door was unlocked so they entered the house. The local FBI office informed the Chicago office.

"Agent Ben Huntsville speaking."

"This is Agent Spencer Davis in Kansas City. I wanted to inform you that we got a hit on that phone number, and it was from a suburban home here. And we have secured the residence. It looks as if they left without packing, so they left in a hurry. I suspect he's going to get rid of that phone since he was almost caught."

Agent Huntsville added, "The Russian, Morris Borkoff, was probably trying to contact Congressman Page. That contact was not successful because we arrested the congressman yesterday and we have his phone. I appreciate the update, and I'll pass it on."

The local law enforcement in Kansas City put out an all-points bulletin for the black limousine and the Russian passengers.

In Chicago, Agent Huntsville called Agent Holly in New Mexico. "This is Agent Ben Huntsville. I want to inform you that the Kansas City office got a hit on that Russian's phone number, and it was from a suburban home there in Kansas City. FBI agents have secured the residence. It looks as if the Russians left without packing, so they left in a hurry. We suspect Morris Borkoff is going to get rid of that phone since he was almost caught. He was trying to contact our prisoner, Congressman Homer Page."

Agent Holly said, "Thank you for the update, and I'll pass it on to the people here who need to know."

Agent Holly called the law enforcement team who happened to be in a meeting in interrogation room one. Acting DA Jefferson put him on speaker so the entire team could get involved. Agent Holly shared all of the information that he had learned from the Chicago office with the team and ended the call.

Acting DA Jefferson analyzed Borkoff's movement. "Let's assess where we are. Since Morris Borkoff had to flee from Kansas City, he's not going to go east because that takes him farther away from Russia. He's headed west, and the closest interstate west from his last-known location is 70."

The team agreed with the assessment.

Acting AD Jefferson called Agent Holly to share their assessment. "This is Acting DA Jefferson speaking. The team and I were just discussing the potential destinations of the Russian, Morris Borkoff. Our theory is that Borkoff wants to get to Russia, so he's not going to travel east. He's heading west. The closest interstate to his last-known location is 70 West. We also believe that he's looking for assistance, and since the Nazi gang has worked with him in the past, they're the most likely to assist him. It's been reported that there is a large contingent of Nazi gang members in Colorado and Utah. So our constructive speculation leads us to deduce that the Russian contacts are in Colorado and Utah. We propose that whatever law enforcement entity has jurisdiction should monitor Nazi activity in that state and also verify the Russian activity in that state."

"I think your team's deductions are concrete, and I will pass it down the line immediately."

"One other thing, we're in close proximity to the targeted state and can assist as needed."

Agent Holly called FBI offices in Chicago, Kansas City, Colorado, and Utah and passed on all of the information that he had received from the New Mexico law enforcement team. They all agreed and were on the lookout for the Russian and Nazi gang's activity.

Agent Holly made a follow-up call to Acting DA Jefferson confirming that FBI offices were in complete agreement with their assessment. He updated the law enforcement team.

"Agent Holly just provided an update on what's occurred since we first informed him of our thoughts on the movement and intent of Morris Borkoff. He made contact with FBI agents in the Colorado and Utah offices. He shared with them our team's constructive speculation and deductive conclusions. Those offices agreed. They also agreed to keep New Mexico law enforcement updated on their process moving forward."

Detective Beckman believed they were closing in on the Russian. "That sounds productive, and maybe it's the trap we need to finally apprehend Morris Borkoff."

Detective Littleton concurred. "I agree with you, Detective Beckman. And that's just right across the border from us, so maybe we should inform our drug task force to be on alert."

Detective Phillips decided to act within his authority. "As acting chief, I have the authority to put our component of the task force on alert. That includes SWAT and city law enforcement. Let me add that this is in conjunction with the existing national all-points bulletin and nationwide manhunt for Morris Borkoff."

Acting DA Jefferson said, "I'm happy to reiterate that based on our ongoing productive dialogue, we have assisted in creating circumstances that I'm convinced terrifies the Russian. Consider what has happened.

His cruise ship lines and nationwide trucking lines are gone, and more importantly, we've incarcerated over five hundred of his men. He had a congressman and a police chief in his pocket, and now they're locked up. We have his assets frozen, and he's been reduced to a felon running for his life."

Detective Phillips shared his projections. "If you're on 70 West and you're trying to catch a boat to Russia, you have to get to the ocean as quickly as possible. He's got to try to catch Interstate 15, which would take him to San Diego."

Acting DA Jefferson inquired, "What boats are departing San Diego that could take him to Russia?"

Detective Beckman said, "That sounds like another assignment for the FBI."

Detective Phillips added, "We know this guy does not want to go close to Los Angeles or San Francisco because he's red-hot there. I believe he thinks he can fly under the radar in San Diego because the drug bust didn't occur in that city. He may have a special ship coming in to help him. And you have to remember he's pressed for time. We're closing in on this guy. And he has to be desperate because he could get trapped against the ocean in San Diego."

Acting DA Jefferson called the FBI. "This is Acting DA Robert Jefferson. The team believes Morris Borkoff is focusing on the intersection of Interstate 70 and Interstate 15. We believe that he's trying to get to the ocean as quickly as possible. And our projections suggest that he will continue to the intersection of Interstate 70 and Interstate 15 and continue southwest on Interstate 15 to San Diego. The ocean is his goal. This could also be an opportunity to identify the Russian's present location. Any cell phone discussion concerning that route should receive scrutiny. We suspect that the Russian will attempt to move through the night and get on a boat in San Diego."

Agent Holly said, "I'll pass this on to Agent Mike Dupree immediately."

Agent Holly conference-called Agents Mike Dupree in the Utah office and John Johnson in the Colorado office. He informed them of the New Mexico team's projections relating to the intersection of Interstates 70 and 15, with the port in San Diego being Morris Borkoff's projected destination. Their projections included cell phone coordination by the Russian with whoever was going to pick him up in San Diego. That coordination could also include interaction by phone or in person with Nazis or Russians in Colorado and Utah.

"If we can identify cell phone discussion pertaining to that route and destination, it could also be an opportunity to identify the Russian's present location. Any cell phone discussion relating to that route should receive scrutiny. The team suspects that the Russian will attempt to move through the night and get on a boat in San Diego."

Agent Dupree sent emails to FBI offices in Arizona, California, and Nevada, sharing the news. Meanwhile, the Russian, Morris Borkoff, was feeling the pressure of the nationwide manhunt, and as a result, he was trying to get to Utah where he knew there were Russians and Nazis that would assist him at evading law enforcement. But what he didn't know was that Utah law enforcement, including FBI, SWAT, state, county, and city components, were monitoring Russian and Nazi activity.

The Russian had secured a new cell phone, just as law enforcement had projected, and he called his contacts in Colorado.

"This is Nic speaking."

"This is Morris. Will see you soon."

Morris Borkoff and his companions stopped in Colorado for rest, and they were joined there by a van carrying six Russians and two cars carrying an additional eight Nazis. They were not going down without a fight.

Morris Borkoff shared his plans. "When we get to the intersection of Interstate 70 and Interstate 15, if there are any police there, I want your squad to eliminate them. Once they're eliminated, go north on Interstate 15. Where's that map? Here it is. As soon as possible, get off the interstate on 40 in Provo and dump the van as soon as possible."

Nic Vodka was concerned about Borkoff's safety. "Are you going to be ok with these damn Nazis?"

"Of course you give them money and drugs, and they'll be your slaves for life."

Both men laughed. The Russian and his escorts were traveling westward on Interstate 70, swiftly approaching the intersection of Interstate 70 and Interstate 15. While the word had gone out among law enforcement that this was an important intersection, it was lightly guarded. There were two police cars, with two officers per car, one car parked on the south side of the intersection and the other parked on the north side of the intersection.

The officers were not expecting a convoy. They were expecting just a black limousine, and they were caught off guard. The van was leading the convoy, and there were six Russians inside. They all had AR-15s. When the van got to the intersection, it came to a sudden stop, and the armed men leaped out of the van, military style, on each side and opened fire on the officers' vehicles.

Pop! Pop! Pop! Pop! Pop! Pop! Pop! Pop! Pop! Pop! Pop! Pop! Pop! Pop! Pop! Pop! Pop! Pop! Pop! Pop! Pop! Pop! Pop! Pop! Pop! Pop! Pop! Pop! Pop! Pop! Pop! Pop! Pop! Pop! Pop! Pop! Pop! Pop! Pop! Pop! Pop! Pop! Pop! Pop! Pop! Pop! Pop! Pop! Pop! Pop! Pop! Pop! Pop!

The officers and the civilian traffic didn't have a chance. All four officers were killed and didn't have time to call for help before the shooting started. Also several civilians were killed. After the shooting, the van left the scene traveling north on Interstate 15, and the Russian's limousine and two support vehicles, with six armed Nazis in each car, proceeded south on Interstate 15.

Acting DA Jefferson got a call from Agent Holly. "This is Agent Holly. I wanted to inform you that four Utah state troopers and several civilians were killed by six armed men in a van at the intersection of Interstate 70 and Interstate 15. Your deductions were absolutely correct."

"Were any witnesses able to see which direction the vehicles traveled after the shooting?"

"They saw the gray van traveling north on Interstate 15. No one noticed the direction of the black limousine."

"Remind everyone to stay focused on Interstate 15 South. The Russian is trying to get to San Diego."

Acting DA Jefferson informed the team. "That was Agent Holly, and he had good and bad news."

Detective Phillips was seeking clarity. "What do you mean?"

"We were right about the intersection at Interstate 70 and Interstate 15. They just had a shootout there, and four state troopers and several civilians were killed."

Detective Beckman was frustrated. "Got-damn! Did they see the Russian?"

Acting DA Jefferson shared what he knew. "The only thing that the witnesses reported is that some men jumped out of a van and started shooting at the police cars. When the shooting was over, the van drove north on Interstate 15."

Detective Littleton remarked, "No one saw the damn black limousine?"

"No, they didn't see it. I told Agent Holly to tell law enforcement to keep an eye on Interstate 15 South because the Russian is still trying to get home."

Dianne Jackson kept the team focused. "We need to focus on our backup plan."

Detective Phillips agreed. "You're right. Where's the map?"

Meanwhile the Russians in the van, traveling north on Interstate 15, reached the exit at Highway 40 and headed east back to Colorado. Nic Vodka, the leader in the van, called a contact in Colorado to meet them so they could get out of the gray van.

Ego Alkali answered the call. "You are speaking to Ego."

"This is Nic. I'm on Highway 40 heading for the Colorado line. I need to get out of this van. Come and pick us up."

"I'm coming now."

Back in New Mexico, the law enforcement team continued their work.

Detective Phillips was reading the map. "So if the Russian is traveling southwest on Interstate 15, there are three intersections before you get to San Diego. The first intersection is at Interstate 15 and Highways 95 and 93. The second intersection is at Interstate 15 and Interstate 40. And the third intersection is at Interstate 15 and Interstate 10. That's three chances before the Russian gets to the ocean in San Diego."

Acting DA Jefferson agreed with Phillips' assessment. "Good job, Phillips. We've got to get this information to the FBI right now."

He then made a call to the FBI. "This is Acting DA Jefferson, and I'm calling regarding some additional projections on future contact opportunities to stop the Russian. The Russian is traveling southwest, and there are three intersections where we can stop him before he gets to San Diego. The first intersection is at Interstate 15 and Highways 95 and 93. The second intersection is at Interstate 15 and Interstate 40. And the third intersection is at Interstate 15 and Interstate 10. That's three chances before the Russian gets to the ocean in San Diego. Also the Coast Guard should be alerted of the potential escape attempt at the San Diego harbor."

Agent Holly documented all the details. "I'll get this into the right hands immediately."

Agent Holly sent a high-priority email to FBI offices in Utah, Arizona, California, Nevada, and Colorado. The email content included all of the recent information received from the New Mexico team.

An hour or so later on Interstate 15, Morris Borkoff, traveling in his limousine with his two escort cars, noticed a law enforcement checkpoint at the intersection of Interstate 15 and Interstate 40.

Borkoff called his lead escort, Bubba. "This is Borkoff speaking. I need you to take out that checkpoint so I can take that Interstate 40."

Borkoff called the second escort, John Buford, which was behind his car. "Morris Borkoff speaking. The law has a roadblock so we're going to have to go back to Interstate 93 and make a right. Bubba is going to attack the police to give us time to turn around."

John Buford was ready for a fight. "I can help Bubba and then catch up to you."

"All right. When you're done here, call me, and I'll tell you where we'll meet up."

The men in the lead escort car got their AR-15s ready, and as they got closer to the checkpoint, where four police cars were blocking the exit with two officers per car, they rolled down the windows and opened fire.

Pop! Pop! Pop! Pop! Pop! Pop! Pop! Pop! Pop! Pop! Pop! Pop!
Pop! Pop! Pop! Pop! Pop! Pop! Pop! Pop! Pop! Pop! Pop! Pop! Pop!
Pop! Pop! Pop! Pop! Pop! Pop! Pop! Pop! Pop! Pop! Pop! Pop!
Pop! Pop!

The officers returned fire. As the shootout started, Morris Borkoff's driver crossed the median and headed the limousine north on Interstate 15. One of the state troopers was able to radio for help.

"This is car eighty-seven, and we're at the checkpoint at Interstate 15 and Interstate 40 intersection. We're under heavy weapons fire. Need support immediately. The black limousine just headed north on Interstate 15."

After killing three troopers and wounding four, the two cars crossed the median and headed north on Interstate 15 with several state trooper vehicles in hot pursuit.

Bubba Dotson called John Buford. "John, we need to go back to 93 and make a right!"

"I thought we were going to take 40!"

"Hell, no way we could have moved them cop cars. The Russian is headed to 93, so let's hit it!"

As the two criminal vehicles approached Exit 93, they saw that multiple law enforcement vehicles had blocked the exit.

John Buford called Bubba Dotson. "This is John. What the hell are we going to do, Bubba? The law got our exit blocked!"

"We're going to have to cross the median again and head back south. Let's go!"

The criminals crossed the median again, and they saw several law enforcement vehicles in their front and rear with blue lights flashing and sirens sounding. They were trapped! They stopped their cars and started to get out with their hands up. They were all handcuffed and read their rights.

Meanwhile Morris Borkoff's vehicle had taken the Highway 93 exit prior to the law enforcement blockade and was headed for Interstate 40 East.

Morris Borkoff made a call to Nic. "This is Morris. Are you ok?"

"We switched vans when we got to Colorado, so we're safe. What about you?"

"I'm on Highway 93 approaching Interstate 40 East. They cut me off before I could get to the ocean. Can you get to me?"

"I can meet you in New Mexico."

"I can't go to Albuquerque. What about Lordsburg? Just take Interstate 25 down to Interstate 10 and make a right!"

"We're on the way."

Three white vans left Denver, heading to Lordsburg, New Mexico, to save the drug boss.

In New Mexico, Agent Holly made a call to Acting DA Jefferson. "This is Agent Holly, and thanks to your team's accurate information, law enforcement officials were able to prevent Morris Borkoff from getting on that boat. There was some shooting, and we lost three state troopers, but at least we stopped him."

"Where's Morris Borkoff right now? Does anybody know?"

"He's actually in your area. California law enforcement believes he escaped off Interstate 15 onto Highway 93 traveling southeast in that black limousine."

"Thanks for the update."

Acting DA Jefferson shared the news with the team. "Guess what? Morris Borkoff missed his boat."

Detective Littleton said, "That's the type of news we like around here!"

The team started high-fiving each other.

Acting DA Jefferson continued, "That's not all. We believe he escaped arrest by exiting Interstate 15 onto Highway 93 traveling southeast, which means he's in our neighborhood."

Detective Phillips wanted to identify possible points of contact. "Where's that map? He's not going to want to come through Albuquerque. I'm going to call dispatch right now."

After they picked up, he said, "This is Acting Chief Virgil Phillips. We need a statewide all-points bulletin for the Russian, Morris Borkoff. Last seen traveling in a black limousine on Highway 93 in Arizona traveling toward Interstate 40. He's fleeing California law enforcement.

He's traveling with at least three or four others. He may have secured additional help. He's very dangerous. Approach with caution."

Dispatch immediately sent out the all-points bulletin. The law enforcement team was still meeting, attempting to figure out the Russian's next move.

Acting DA Jefferson continued, "So we don't think he's coming to Albuquerque. Where do we think he's going?"

The acting chief made projections. "We need roadblocks at Interstate 40 and Interstate 10. We also need roadblocks on Highways 60 and 180. That will cover everything entering the state from the west and traveling east. I'll call it in."

He made the call to dispatch. Dispatch sent out the instructions.

"Acting Chief Virgil Phillips is requesting roadblocks at the western border of the state at Interstates 40 and 10 and Highways 60 and 180. Repeat: this is a statewide all-points bulletin for the Russian, Morris Borkoff. Last seen traveling in a black limousine on Highway 93 traveling toward Interstate 40 East. He's fleeing California law enforcement. He's traveling with three or four others. He may have secured additional help. He's very dangerous. Approach with caution."

Meanwhile, Morris Borkoff was traveling without escort, but things were about to change because there were three van loads of Russians headed to Lordsburg, New Mexico, to rescue him.

Morris Borkoff got a call. "This is Morris. Nic, where are you?"

"We're leaving Albuquerque and heading your way. It's going to be approximately seven and a half hours before we're there. Where are you?"

Morris Borkoff said, "We spent the night at a hotel in Globe, Arizona. That's about three hours from our destination. There's going to be roadblocks somewhere, but I don't know where yet."

"I will see you soon."

That morning at the Globe Hotel, one of Morris Borkoff's bodyguards looked out of his hotel room window and saw two police officers examining the limousine. He picked up his AR-15 and rushed out the door, and a gunfight ensued.

Officer Douglas yelled a warning, "Look out! That guy's got a gun!"

The bodyguard fired.

Pop! Pop! Pop! Pop! Pop! Pop! Pop! Pop! Pop! Pop! Pop!

A police officer office was shot as Officer Douglas pulled his handgun, aimed at the shooter, and fired.

Pop! Pop! Pop! Pop! Pop!

The bodyguard yelled, "Oh, I'm hit!" The bodyguard went down.

The second bodyguard fired his AR-15 from the hotel room doorway.

Pop! Pop! Pop! Pop! Pop! Pop! Pop! Pop! Pop! Pop! Pop!

And the second officer went down.

"Let's go!" the bodyguard shouted.

The driver, Natasha Pam, Morris Borkoff, and the bodyguard rushed out of their rooms, and all four got in the limousine and rushed away on Highway 70 Southeast.

Two more police cars arrived at the hotel and called in what they found. "There's been a shooting at Highway 70 Hotel in Globe, Arizona. Two officers and a civilian are down. We need medical support immediately!"

An emergency medical team and additional police sped to the crime scene. A statewide call went out from the Globe police force.

Dispatch announced, "Be on alert. This is a statewide and surrounding areas alert. Two police officers and one Russian national have been killed in a shootout at the Highway 70 hotel in Globe, Arizona. The Globe police force believes that some of the Russians got away in a black limousine. The local police believe that these are the Russians wanted in a nationwide manhunt."

Agent Holly made a call to Acting DA Jefferson. "This is Agent Holly. Twenty minutes ago, there was a gunfight in Globe, Arizona, at the Highway 70 hotel. Two police officers and a Russian national was killed. Four people escaped in a black limousine believed to be heading east."

"It sounds like a single car traveling alone."

"That's correct. If they have help coming, it apparently hasn't arrived yet."

"We've got every western entry into the state blocked, so if he shows up, we're going to get him."

Acting DA Jefferson immediately shared what he just learned from the FBI. "That was Agent Holly. He confirmed what we'd heard from the Globe police."

The continued loss of colleagues upset Detective Littleton. "That bastard is still killing our people."

Detective Beckman added, "That's why they call it a drug war. Any minute someone can die."

Acting Chief Phillips focused on the mission. "Is there anything else we can do to guarantee the successful arrest of this criminal?"

Dianne Jackson made an observation. "It looks like he is trying to slip in on Highway 70, but he's been discovered. So what's his backup plan?"

Acting Chief Phillips was using the map. "He's so close to that southern border of both Arizona and New Mexico that he can't get back to Interstate 40. There's too much of a law enforcement presence to try to travel north. He's traveling east for a reason. He can't go south because of the ocean. He's trapped! What's the closest town between Globe, Arizona, and our western border on Highway 70?"

Detective Littleton remarked, "That would be Lordsburg, New Mexico."

Acting DA Jefferson said, "That's their target, which makes it our target."

Acting Chief Phillips called dispatch. "This is Acting Chief Phillips. I need the statewide and surrounding areas for Morris Borkoff to be updated to include most likely the landing target of Lordsburg, New Mexico. Proceed with caution. He may have assistance. Also include a request for air support for the Lordsburg area. Send that out immediately."

Dispatch announced, "This is a priority alert to all units at and near Lordsburg, New Mexico. Lordsburg is the suspected targeted entry point for the Russian, Morris Borkoff. Proceed with caution. Borkoff may be assisted by others. Air support is requested for the Lordsburg area."

Meanwhile, Morris Borkoff and his group were traveling along Highway 70 close to the New Mexico western border, and they saw the roadblock. Morris Borkoff called Nic Vodka.

"This is Morris. Where are you?"

"I'm ten minutes east of Lordsburg. Where are you?"

"I'm just west of the New Mexico border, and there's a roadblock that's keeping me from getting to Lordsburg. I may have to turn around and take Highway 191."

"I've got twenty-one men, and we're armed with AR-15s and grenades. We can bust that roadblock."

"When you bust it, we've got to get on Highway 10 East."

"I see the roadblock, and it's time to go to work. Talk to you in a few minutes."

The vans drove up to the roadblock, and four men jumped out and began throwing grenades at the police officers and their vehicles.

Boom! Boom! Boom! Boom! Boom! Boom! Boom! Boom!

The officers didn't expect a grenade attack. The officers hurriedly took cover and started shooting as the Russian mobsters returned fire and continued tossing grenades.

Pop! Pop! Pop! Pop! Pop! Pop! Pop! Pop! Pop! Pop! Pop! Pop! Pop! Pop! Pop! Pop! Pop! Pop! Pop! Pop! Pop! Pop! Pop! Pop! Pop! Pop! Pop! Pop! Pop! Pop! Pop! Pop! Pop! Pop! Pop! Pop! Pop! Pop! Pop! Pop! Pop! Pop! Pop! Pop! Pop! Boom! Boom! Boom! Boom! Boom! Boom! Boom! Boom!

In the confusion during the battle, one of the vans, driven by Nic Vodka, got around the roadblock as the occupants of the other two vans continued the gun battle with people dying on both sides.

Pop! Pop! Pop! Pop! Pop! Pop! Pop! Pop! Pop! Pop! Pop! Pop! Pop! Pop! Pop! Pop! Pop! Pop! Boom!

Nic Vodka's van drove northwest on Highway 70 until he spotted Morris Borkoff's limousine. Borkoff, Natasha Pam, his driver, and bodyguard abandoned the limousine and joined Vodka and four others in the van. They headed north on Arizona Highway 191. After hearing gunfire and explosions at the nearby Highway 70 roadblock, the law enforcement officials at the Interstate 10 roadblock rushed to assist their colleagues at the Highway 70 roadblock.

Pop! Pop! Pop! Pop! Pop! Pop! Pop! Pop! Pop! Pop! Pop! Pop! Pop! Pop! Pop! Pop! Pop! Pop! Boom!

The gunfight at the Highway 70 roadblock was over. Out of seventeen Russians that were there, only four were alive. And seven law enforcement officials were dead. While Morris Borkoff might have escaped capture, law enforcement killed thirteen Russians and captured four. They also had two white vans with Colorado license plates. It was now night, and the third van, loaded with Russians, was on Arizona Highway 191, heading north.

Morris Borkoff used a throwaway phone and made a phone call to Ego. "This is Morris."

"You made it. I'm glad!"

"Listen, we're on Highway 191 approaching Utah. I need you to take Interstate 70 west and then take Highway 191 and pick us up in Utah. There are nine of us in this van, and we need you now."

"Don't worry. I'm on the way."

In Rifle, Colorado, Ego Alkali locked the door to his home, got in a black van, and headed down Interstate 70 West. He was on the way to meet his boss, Morris Borkoff.

Later that day, the law enforcement team was having a planning session, and Acting DA Jefferson made the opening statement.

"I wanted us to assess the results of today's effort. As we all know, there was a shootout at the Highway 70 roadblock on our western border. Three vans approached the roadblock from the east off Interstate 10. Approximately twenty Russians used AR-15s and grenades in a battle that lasted a couple of hours. And if law enforcement from the Interstate 10 roadblock hadn't assisted, the Highway 70 roadblock battle would have been lost. Out of seventeen Russians that we accounted for, only four are alive. And seven law enforcement officials are dead. While

Morris Borkoff did escape capture, we did capture two white vans with Colorado license plates. Those numbers are 999-0097 and 999-0098."

Detective Beckman shared her thoughts. "It sounds like he's got a stronghold in Colorado."

"Good point, Detective Beckman. Let me call the FBI."

Acting DA Jefferson called Agent Holly. "This is Acting DA Jefferson. The Russians use vans from Carson's Van Rentals from Denver. Those van license plate numbers are 999-0097 and 999-0098."

"I'll pass it on immediately."

After receiving the van information, the FBI in Denver was at Carson's Van Rentals to discuss the three vans the Russians used to commit capital murder in New Mexico. They entered, showed their badges, and introduced themselves.

"I'm FBI Agent John Johnson, and this is FBI Agent Bob Dickson. We're here to get information about three vans that you leased or rented within the last week. Here's the license numbers on two of the three: 999-0097 and 999-0098."

The attendant, Jeffery Smith, looked up the rental record. "I'm going to have to talk to my manger about this. Just a moment." The attendant walked down the hall to Bill McMaster's office.

"Bill, there's two FBI agents here to discuss some of our van rentals." He handed Bill McMaster the document with the license plate numbers.

"Tell them to come on back."

The attendant returned to the front counter. "You can go down the hall, and it's the second door on the left."

The agents proceeded down the hall to Bill McMaster's office.

"Come on in and have a seat. Now what can I do for you?"

The agents showed their badges. "I'm FBI Agent John Johnson, and this is FBI Agent Bob Dickson. We're here to get information about three vans that you leased or rented within the last week. Here's the license numbers on two of the three: 999-0097 and 999-0098. Those vans were used in the killing of several law enforcement officers. And as a result, we're conducting a capital murder investigation. Who is the person, or persons, that you leased or rented those vans to? And before you answer, it's my duty to inform you that making false statements to an investigator during an official investigation is a crime."

"Agent Johnson, I have no intentions of making false statements, but we do have a policy of not giving out information on our customers. Considering the seriousness of the investigation, I don't foresee any problem getting this information for you. I do need to consult our attorney prior to doing so to make sure I do it properly."

"The FBI respects your need to comply with your company's policy, but the agency would appreciate a timely response to our request."

"I understand. Let me make a phone call."

Bill McMaster called his attorney, Jeff E. Wilson. "Jeff, this is Bill. I've got two FBI agents in my office wanting to know personal information on some of our customers. I told them I wanted to talk to you before releasing anything to make sure I'm complying with our legal responsibilities. Let me add that according to the FBI, our vans were used in a homicide where law enforcement officers were killed. Before you answer, I'm going to put you on speaker."

Jeff Wilson understood the seriousness of the circumstances. "Yes, Bill. Release the information immediately."

"Thank you, Jeff, and have a great day."

Bill McMaster made another call to his attendant. "Jeffery, this is Bill. Make copies of all three of those lease agreements for the FBI."

"I'll do it right away."

"Jeffery is getting that information for you, and he should have it ready in a minute or two."

Agent Johnson said, "We appreciate your cooperation."

The agents left Bill McMaster's office, went back to the front counter, and waited for the material.

"Here's that information you requested, and that third van license plate number is 999-0099. If we can do anything else, just let us know."

The FBI agents left the business, got in their car, and headed back to their office. After arriving at the office, they prepared an application for a warrant to wiretap the phones of Carson's Van Rentals and the home and cell phones of Bill McMaster. The agents emailed copies of the leasing documents to the FBI office in New Mexico to Agent Holly, who forwarded them to the law enforcement team. The FBI also sent out a nationwide alert on the third van involved in the shootout in New Mexico, including the van license plate number, 999-0099.

At the FBI New Mexico office, Agent Holly made a call to Acting DA Jefferson. "This is Agent Holly. The FBI Denver office just provided the leasing documents for those three vans used by the Russians in that gunfight the other day. I'm going to email them to you right now."

"Thanks, Agent Holly. I look forward to receiving them."

The law enforcement team was in the middle of a planning meeting.

Acting DA Jefferson continued, "That was Agent Holly, and he had some good news. The FBI Denver office obtained the leasing documents on those three vans used in the gunfight the other day."

Detective Phillips said, "That's the type of break in this case we need."

Detective Littleton added, "This time when we find those damn Russians, we're going to get them even if we have to go to Denver ourselves to do it."

At that moment Acting DA Jefferson's secretary knocked on the door, opened it, and handed him copies of the leasing documents, and she left and closed the door. Acting DA Jefferson passed out copies. The team studied the documents.

Acting DA Jefferson commented, "Carson's Van Rentals license plate numbers on the three vans are 999-0097, 999-0098, and 999-0099."

Detective Beckman said, "I hope the FBI has tapped Carson's phones."

Detective Phillips replied, "That'll be easy to confirm, but we need to focus on Morris Borkoff's next move. He still wants to get out of the country."

Acting DA Jefferson shared his observation. "These documents are fraudulent. This signature for Bubba Dotson is no good because he was in jail at the time these vans were rented. Let's double-check to make sure. I'm going to give the FBI a call."

Once Agent Holly picked up, he said, "This is Acting DA Robert Jefferson. We've just discovered that the signature on these leasing documents have to be fraudulent because it indicates Bubba Dotson was the signee. But at the time the vans were leased, Bubba Dotson was in jail. We believe that he'd been arrested in California for participating in a shootout connected to the Russian, Morris Borkoff."

"If they're not aware, I'll make sure that the Denver office knows of the potential fraud."

Agent Holly then called the FBI Denver office. "Agent Johnson speaking."

"This is Agent Holly. Our law enforcement team and Acting DA Robert Jefferson just discovered what they believe to be a fraudulent signature on the Carson's Rental Vans leasing documents. The documents indicate that Bubba Dotson was the signee. It appears that at the time the vans were leased, Bubba Dotson was in jail. He'd been arrested in California for participating in a shootout connected to the Russian, Morris Borkoff."

Agent Johnson said, "Thank you for that insight. We'll do our due diligence and respond accordingly." He then called California State Police.

"Captain El Sanchez speaking."

"This is FBI Agent John Johnson in the Denver office. I'm calling to verify the arrest of a man at a state police checkpoint at Interstate 15 and Interstate 40 intersection. Bubba Dotson."

"Yeah, I remember that shootout. It was a tough one. I'm in our database, and yes, we did arrest Bubba Dotson for capital murder. We've had him locked up for approximately two weeks."

"That's very helpful because there were some vans used to help the Russian escape a checkpoint in New Mexico four days ago, and the vans were supposedly leased to Bubba Dotson. I believe it's the same guy because of the Russian connection in each altercation. You've been extremely helpful. Thank you."

Agent Johnson emailed Agent Holly, confirming that Bubba Dotson was incarcerated in California at the time those vans were leased in Denver. Agent Holly forwarded the email to Acting DA Robert Jefferson, who shared the information with the team.

"That's a confirmation from the FBI that Bubba Dotson was incarcerated in California at the time those vans were leased in Denver."

Detective Littleton said, "That's my kind of news."

Detective Phillips added, "They're going to press that van dealer."

The following day, Agents Johnson and Dickson returned to Carson's Van Rentals to discuss the three vans the Russians used to commit capital murder in New Mexico. They entered, showed their badges, and reintroduced themselves to the attendant.

Agents Johnson instructed, "We need to talk to Bill McMaster."

The attendant walked down the hall to Bill McMaster's office. The door was open. "The FBI is back, and they want to talk to you."

The two men walked back to the front counter.

Bill McMaster asked, "What can I do for you today?"

Agent Johnson said, "We need you to come to the FBI office to answer some questions about those vans rented to Bubba Dotson."

"Is there a problem?"

"It would probably be a good idea to call your attorney and have him meet you at our office."

Bill McMaster called his attorney before getting in the back seat of the FBI vehicle and headed to the FBI Denver office. When his attorney, Jeff E. Wilson, arrived at the FBI office, his client was sitting in an interrogation room with two agents, and he joined them. All the men were seated, and they began the discussion.

The attorney asked, "So why is my client here?"

Agent Dickson laid the rental documents on the table and began questioning Bill McMaster. "Do you recall providing us with these documents?"

"Yes, I do."

"These documents indicate that you rented the van to Bubba Dotson. This man was in jail in California at the time these vans were rented. How do you explain that?"

"The man must have had ID because we require that from all of our customers."

"What type of ID do you require?"

"We require a driver's license and proof of insurance."

"Do you take pictures of the documentation?"

"Yes, we do."

"But you didn't include that information when you gave us the van rental documents. Why not?"

Bill McMaster started to get very nervous. "My attendant may have just made a mistake."

"Are you willing to have him bring that entire file, including driver's license information and proof of insurance, here right now?"

"Yes, I will." Bill McMaster called his attendant and requested that he bring the complete files relating to vans 999-0097, 999-0098, and 999-0099.

While they waited on the file, Agent Johnson called Captain El Sanchez and requested a photo of Bubba Watson. Captain Sanchez emailed the photo. Agent Johnson printed a copy and returned to the interrogation room.

When Jeffery Smith arrived at FBI headquarters, he was escorted to the interrogation room. He handed the file to Bill McMaster, who opened the folder, took out the photo copies, and told Jeffery Smith he could leave.

Agent Johnson said, "While we were waiting on your information, I had the state police send me a picture of Bubba Dotson."

They compared the state police photo with the driver's license photo. It was not a match.

Bill McMaster said, "I don't know how this happened. I don't watch over my staff every minute of the day."

Agent Johnson asked, "Have you ever done business with any Russians prior to this van rental? I'm going to remind you again that your vans were used in the killing of several law enforcement officers. And as a result, we're conducting a capital murder investigation. Who is the person, or persons, that you leased or rented those vans to? And before you answer, it's my duty to inform you again that making false statements to an investigator during an official investigation is a crime."

"All types of people lease my vans. And the ID that he provided is all that I have."

"You didn't answer my question."

"I may have done business with Russians in the past."

"We need all of your files on your Russian customers. And we need those now."

Meanwhile, the law enforcement team in New Mexico was in a strategy session when the facts started to fall into place.

Acting DA Jefferson said, "The owner of Carson's Van Rentals is Bill McMaster. That name just keeps ringing in my ears."

Detective Phillips replied, "He's connected to Russians through his vehicle business. So what other vehicle businesses are tied to the Russians?"

Detective Littleton answered, "Trucking companies."

Acting DA Jefferson said, "That's it! Where are the files on the trucking line that was shipping the heroin?"

Detective Beckman replied, "Here's that file."

Acting DA Jefferson added, "This is it! The guy that owns the van rental, Bill McMaster, has the same last name as the guy that owns Big Freeze Trucking Line, George McMaster. I have to call the FBI right now!"

Once Agent Holly picked up, he said, "This is Acting DA Jefferson. We have some hot information. The owner of the Denver Carson's Van Rental business that were used in the shootout here, Bill McMaster, has the exact last name as the owner of the Big Freeze Trucking Line, George McMaster. As you know, they were receiving the heroin off the Russian cruise ships onto their trucks."

"Hot damn! Let me make a call to Denver right now. Thanks!"

Agent Holly called Agent Johnson in Denver. "Agent Holly here. The owner of the Denver-based Carson's Van Rental business that were used in the shootout here, Bill McMaster, has the exact last name as the owner of the Big Freeze Trucking Line owner, George McMaster. They were receiving the heroin off the Russian cruise ships onto their trucks, and they are in prison in New Mexico. There could be a family history of working with Russians!"

"That's great news. He's in my interrogation room at this very moment. Thank you so much, and I'll keep you updated."

Agent Johnson continued the questioning of Bill McMaster. "Are you familiar with George McMaster, the owner of the Big Freeze Trucking Line?"

Bill McMaster was slow to respond. "George is my brother."

"Are you co-owner of that trucking line?"

His attorney said, "I'd like to have a word with my client."

Agents Johnson and Dickson stepped out into the corridor to allow Bill McMaster time to speak with his attorney. Agent Johnson shared with Agent Dickson all he had learned during the phone call with Agent Holly.

Meanwhile in the interrogation room, Bill McMaster felt the pressure and was depending on his attorney to guide him through his difficulties. "I'm part owner in that damn trucking line, and my brother is part owner in my rental business. I never had any direct dealings with the heroin, but I have received some Russian money to look the other way on some leasing agreements for my vans."

His attorney said, "Here's the problem. They used your vans in the murder of law enforcement officers. What can you give the FBI?"

"There's a house in Rifle, Colorado, where the Russians hide out."

"Give them up and save yourself and your family."

"If I give them up, they could come after my family. These damn Russians are all over our country, and I don't care how many they lock up. These bastards just keep coming."

"They can offer you and your family protection. If you don't give up the Russians, you're going to be arrested, and you're going to prison for the rest of your life."

"Ok, let's talk to them."

The attorney got up from his seat, walked to the door, opened it, and let the agents know that they were ready to talk.

Bill McMaster continued, "Yes, I'm part owner of the Big Freeze Trucking Line."

Agent Johnson asked, "Did you know that your trucking line was part of a drug trafficking organization?"

"My brother ran the trucking business. I run the van business."

"You didn't answer my question. Did you know that your trucking line was part of a drug trafficking organization?"

Bill McMaster started to cry. "Yes, I knew it."

Agent Johnson continued to apply pressure. "Is your van business part of that same drug trafficking organization?"

"I just rent them vans. I don't know what they do with them. Look, Agent Johnson, I can help you catch this Russian that you are looking for, if you can help me stay out of prison."

"Are you talking about Morris Borkoff?"

"Yeah, that's the one."

"You, your brother, and your Russian associates have caused the deaths of a lot of law enforcement officials."

"But if you protect my wife, kids, and me, I'll hand him to you on a silver platter."

"We'll protect your family, but you may have to do some time. Where is he?"

"I want my family safe."

"Your family has been benefiting from Russian drug money. I'll do what I can for you, but you need to tell me right now where that damn Russian is!"

"There's a ranch house right outside a town named Rifle, Colorado. They use that place to relax, and I figure the Russian has to be worn out the way you guys have been chasing him. And he's got his woman with him so she has to be needing rest too."

Agent Johnson pressed Bill McMaster. "What's the address for the ranch house?"

"Somebody needs to go to my house and bring my family in before you hit the Russians. They will know I talked the minute you show up."

"As soon as we're done with this meeting, Agent Dickson will be in charge of getting your family taken care of. So now tell me the address."

Bill McMaster cried some more as he told the agents what they wanted to know. "7789 Hickory Tree Road. They may have ten to fifteen men there. Maybe twenty."

Later that day inside the ranch house, Morris Borkoff and Natasha Pam were still worn out from being on the run for weeks. Natasha was malnourished and exhausted lying in bed. Morris Borkoff was sitting on the side of the bed and handing her a glass of water, and he attempted to reassure her that they'd make it back to Russia.

"Don't worry, Natasha. We'll leave for Canada in two days, and from there, we'll make our way home."

Natasha Pam was close to a nervous breakdown. "Somehow they always know where we're going, and we nearly die. I can't take any more of the running and hiding."

"We will make it this time. Trust me. I love you."

That night, Agent Johnson and several agents were joined by state, county, and city law enforcement officers outside of the ranch house and were ready to make the arrest.

Agent Johnson talked into a loudspeaker. "This is the FBI. We have your house surrounded on all sides. We have tear gas, and we will use it unless you lay down all of your weapons and come out with your hands up right now!"

Inside the house Natasha Pam was terrified at the sound of the loudspeaker, and she became hysterical. "I can't take it anymore. You lied to me. We're not safe. I'm losing my mind! Go ahead and kill me. Kill me now. I can't run anymore!"

Morris Borkoff was shaken to see her in this condition, and he knew he was responsible. "I'll save you! I'll save you!"

Natasha Pam was crying and pulling her hair. "No, no, no! You can't save me. I'm going to die. You can't help me!"

Law enforcement began a barrage of tear gas. Agent Johnson yelled into loudspeaker, "Fire!"

Boom! Boom! Boom! Boom! Boom! Boom! Boom! Boom! Boom! Boom! Boom! Boom! Boom! Boom! Boom! Boom! Boom!

As the ranch house filled with smoke and none of the occupants could breathe, one of the Russians opened the front door, raised his hands, and walked out. He was soon followed by the rest. The last two to come out were Morris Borkoff carrying Natasha Pam, who had had a nervous breakdown.

The following day the law enforcement team was in their daily strategy session when they got a call from Agent Holly.

"Acting DA Jefferson speaking."

"This is Agent Holly, and I'm happy to report that Morris Borkoff was taken into custody at a ranch house in Rifle, Colorado, at approximately eight fifty-seven Colorado time last night."

Acting DA Jefferson was overjoyed. "Congratulations and thank you."

He shared the news. "Well, team, that was Agent Holly, and I'm happy to tell you that according to his report, Morris Borkoff was taken into custody at a ranch house in Rifle, Colorado, at approximately eight fifty seven Colorado time last night."

They began to high-five and laugh.

Detective Littleton made an offer that no one would refuse. "Let's go to lunch early today. I'm buying!"

The rest of the team was ready to eat. "Sounds good to us!"

They all laughed and headed to lunch.

About the Author

During a 32 year career in Facility Engineering, overseeing Architectural and Engineering design and construction projects, Leonard learned that paying attention to detail is what makes the difference between success or failure. And he brings that attention to detail to each of his fiction writing projects. Whether it's the drama of planning and executing a large scale drug bust or courtroom suspense, Leonard's attention to detail is on display.

Printed in the United States
By Bookmasters